UNLEASHED

A Comic Relief

by

David L. Gersh

OPEN
BOOKS

OTHER BOOKS BY DAVID L. GERSH

Art Is Dead

Going, Going, Gone

Desperate Shop Girls

Art Attack

How to Collect Great Art on a Shoestring

The Whisper of a Distant God

Pot Luck

All's Fair

To Harriette and Bill Cook, who we will never forget.
And, of course, to my wife Anne, without whom
this would not be possible.

Chapter 1

"FLAT AS A PANCAKE," Sal said, shaking his head.

Some towns have a radio station. Some have a newspaper. We have Sal. He's my barber.

Sal's place is gossip central for San Buenasera. At least for those of us who are male. Susie Wilson's hair salon has the women's concession. Sal has been in town so long, he knows everything.

I get my hair trimmed every two weeks. When you're famous, there are standards you need to maintain. My name is James Emerson Harris, and I'm a lawyer.

"They had to scrape poor Rusty Krinik off his driveway," Sal said. "Flat as a pancake," he repeated in a lugubrious tone.

"Golly, that's awful. I hadn't heard."

"Happened yesterday morning."

Sal paused when the door swung open and a large man entered.

"Charlie," Sal said, "take a chair." He gestured towards the man with his scissors. "I'll only be a little bit."

"Damn rain," the man said, removing his hat and shaking it off. He hung it up on a peg on the wall next to the door where it dripped happily onto the linoleum.

I resumed my conversation with Sal.

"What happened?"

"Run over by a steam roller."

Rusty was the mayor of our great town of San Buenasara.

1

"How old was Rusty?"

"Seventy-one."

"That's young," I said. Amazing how your perceptions change as you become wiser with age.

"Too damn young," Charlie interjected, shaking his head, as his lips drew a frown on his face.

"One of my best customers. I saw him last week," Sal added.

"Sal, Rusty was bald," I said.

"Yeah," Sal said, resuming his work with the straight razor, "that's what made him a really terrific customer. A couple of snips over the ears and he was out of the chair. I liked Rusty. I thought he was a good mayor. Solid. Liked things peaceful."

Rusty had been the longest serving mayor in San Buenasara's history. No one had run against him in 20 years. Nobody thought they could win. Nobody wanted to. Everyone liked Rusty. He was a good guy. Besides, it was a lousy job given the yahoos who constituted the rest of our citizens.

Sal's shop has been a fixture in San Buenasera forever. He's the best barber in town. Actually, now, he's the only barber in town since Jesus Corda closed up during the pandemic.

His shop is on Main Street. The business district of San Buenasara consists of three blocks of mismatched one-story buildings with flaking paint, anchored on one end by Sal's and on the other by The Lilly Pad. After Lilly's, Main Street struggles across a little bridge over San Buenasara Creek and ends at Hemming's Hotel and Marina, our gesture to gentility. The realtors call it "The Pointe" and charge more.

Sal's is not a salon. It's a shabby store front with a big glass window. A real, old-fashioned barber shop. There are two cracked leather barber chairs, a ceiling fan and old magazines on the table between the customer chairs where you wait for Sal. The walls had been painted white within my lifetime.

Sal's dog, Bob, was lying across the floor in front of the curtain to the back room. Bob's a nondescript, lovable mutt, with a Golden Retriever somewhere in his genes. He and Bruno are friends.

Bob was with Sal even before Bruno chose to join us. Bruno is our long-haired dachshund.

The shop smelled of aftershave, talcum powder and wet dog. The light was muffled with shadows playing across the floors and walls. There was an occasional flash of sunshine when the clouds took a break from romping across the sky. I was sitting in the chair closest to the window. I could see the dark clouds gathering. Hey, I'm not superstitious. But it couldn't be an omen, could it?

Some people have described San Buenasara as quaint. That's a nice way of saying seedy. We like it that way. It keeps the riff raff in.

Sal is old fashioned too. He doesn't believe in electric gadgets. He's so old fashioned, he's now on the cutting edge of barbering. He uses only a scissors and a comb. There is a little electric clipper for emergencies, but he keeps it hidden. He does the edges and neck with a straight razor that he strops on a thick leather strap that hangs by the side of the chair.

A rotating red and white pole revolves out front. Interesting how that sign came to be. Barbers used to also be surgeons. The person to call if you needed to be bled. A bloody rag, wrapped around a stick became the barber pole.

Sal is a short, wiry guy of Italian heritage, more or less. His skin is brown and leathery. He has a pencil thin mustache which is his pride and joy. No one knows his age, although he looks as old as God. He is always good for a story and a laugh. But now, he looked to be down in the dumps.

The weather kind of matched Sal's mood. It was late August, almost Fall. September wasn't the time for rain. Something had gone wrong. Real wrong. I was going to have to speak to whoever was in charge as soon as I figured out who to talk to.

In San Buenasara, fall usually means 65 degrees and sunny. Not this year. It had been raining incessantly. We were in a rut, and when a rut fills up with water, you call it a river. Great for the drought. But a bit on the weepy side for us. Today was deeply overcast, but our trusty local weather reporter assured us that the rain would let up for a while. Our weatherman is always right.

Sal was using the razor to clean up my sideburns when there was a flash of lightning followed almost immediately by a clap of thunder. Sal yipped and flinched. So did I. Unfortunately, we flinched in different directions. A little pinpoint of blood colored my cheek. Sal grabbed a small towel and used the edge of it to stanch the blood.

He clicked his tongue expressively and muttered something, shaking his head as he reached for a stippling stick.

"Ouch," I complained as he applied the stick vigorously. I jumped and gripped the arms of the barber chair. I'm brave, but I'm tender.

"It won't show, Jimmy. It'll give your face some character." Sal had a peculiar sense of humor. "Just don't stand in any bright light." There was a smile on his face. It is a guiding principle of mine that you never talk back to a man holding a straight razor. It had always served me well.

The rain let go big time and started streaming down the big window out front, leaving a kind of dull, wavering light in the shop.

"Wait a minute, Sal. Did you say he was run over by a steam roller?" I asked, raising my head quickly and risking another visit to the cutting edge.

"Yeah," Charlie said from the wall. "He was."

Was I the last person in town to always hear the news?

"Run over by a damn steamroller," Charlie said with a guffaw.

"Good Lord. I better call Clyde," I said to no one in particular. Clyde is my law partner. He's the best lawyer in San Buenasara. Well, maybe next to me. We are on a long-term retainer to the city as a result of my imprisonment. It wasn't my fault.

"The town is going to be sued." I started to pull off the white cloth Sal had draped on me as I leaned forward in the chair to get up. Sal put his hand on my arm to stop me.

"Nope," he said firmly.

Sal isn't a lawyer. He doesn't understand these things. I, on the other hand, am a master. I would set him straight.

"Sal, if the town is involved in a fatal accident, there is almost always a lawsuit by the family."

"Yeah, I know, but Rusty didn't have any close family."

"Then by his estate." I got him there.

Sal took a left turn in our conversation.

"No one was driving," he said.

My eyes widened. This was incredible. Run down by a city steam roller with no one driving. A negligent steam roller. Talk about a tough case to defend. How do you put a steam roller on the stand? The only good part of it was that the steamroller was unlikely to have been drinking.

This one was going to tax even Clyde's legal genius. Clyde never loses. Except, of course, my murder case. You know, the reason I was in jail. But I've forgiven him for that.

"What happened?" I asked with a querulous tone, leaning back again in the chair. I worked hard to keep my voice down. "How could no one be driving?"

"It was Rusty's steam roller."

"The mayor had his own steam roller?" That was a new perk.

"Jimmy, Rusty loved that steam roller. It was real old. Maybe from the '30s. He bought it from the town. It was the town's first one. Rusty was very proud of it. He had it restored. New paint, everything. He kept it on a stand at the top of his driveway. Polished it every week."

"And one day, it decided to roll over him?"

"It slipped off its stand."

"How could it slip off its stand?"

"No idea."

"Was anyone there?"

"Don't know. Didn't hear of anyone."

"Me neither," said Charlie, eager to be a part of the conversation.

"Will there be an investigation?" I asked.

"Chief Carsone went out to Rusty's already." Sal replied. "Said it looked like an accident to him. Wrapped it up in an hour or two."

Chief Carsone and I have a checkered past. He's not one of my great fans. Probably because I don't think he's too bright and may

5

have mentioned it to him.

"But that was yesterday. What kind of investigation is that? How can he be so sure."

"Said the brakes gave out. Old machine."

"Wow, that is bad timing. The brakes gave out suddenly when Rusty was standing in front of the steam roller."

"Facing the other way."

"You're kidding."

"Nope. They found what was left of him pointed downhill."

"That's fortuitous. Didn't he hear anything? You would think he would turn around."

"Doesn't seem so. Chief Carsone says he was hard of hearing."

"Rusty didn't wear hearing aids, did he?"

"Nope. I would have noticed them when I clipped the hair growing in his ears. Part of my service," Sal said with a touch of pride.

"So Carsone must know something we don't."

"Seems like it." Sal put down the razor and picked up his scissors. He started making small clips here and there.

"What happened to the steam roller?"

"Don't know." Sal must have been really upset. I had never known him to not know so much.

"Know that Chief Carsone hauled it away. Spoke to Sid." Sid is a policeman on our little police force. "Carsone told him it was evidence."

"Where did he take it?"

"Well, it isn't in the parking lot at the police station, that's for sure. Sid didn't know either." Sal stopped snipping and looked over at Charlie. "Charlie, you hear anything?"

"Nope, not a thing."

Sal nodded, then leaned forward and resumed clipping.

"Only know they're getting ready to bury Rusty. At least what's left. Maybe could have a flat coffin? Save some real money."

My mind boggled at the image. Maybe Sal's sense of humor had overcome him. I looked in the mirror to see if he was smirking.

He was dead serious, no pun intended.

"No, Sal, they won't. When's the funeral?" I said firmly.

"Day after tomorrow."

Sal held a mirror up in front of me so I could admire his work. I thought I looked exactly as I did when I came in. Perfect.

"I guess we're going to have to elect a new mayor," I speculated. "Rusty must have over a year left on his term."

"Can't say." He unbuttoned the cloth draped over me and shook it off.

"I wonder how they are going to get someone?"

"Don't know." I may have exhausted Sal's knowledge base. I know I was exhausted.

I got up from the chair and pushed in my shirt. It always rides up when I have a haircut. Bob, the dog, rose with some effort and lumbered over for a scratch. He nosed my leg. I gave him a cursory tug on his ears. I had other places to go.

I knew who would know. There was only one small problem. My office was six blocks away. Karen had taken the car to San Luis Obispo. And I didn't have an umbrella.

Sal grabbed a broom and started to sweep up the hair around the chair. Then he took his white sheet off the arm of the chair and snapped it in Charlie's direction.

"Right nasty out there," Charlie said as he rose and made his way to Sal's barber chair.

At least we all knew that.

I figured I could stop at Polly's and see what he had heard. Polly's store is two doors down from Sal's. I think of Polly's as the center of town. His store is named Pussy Galore, which gives you some idea of why it is so popular with those of us of the male persuasion, although Polly has been trying to expand his market.

I opened Sal's door a crack, slipped out and made a dash for it. I hoped it might stop raining while I talked to Polly.

He wasn't there. And it didn't.

Chapter 2

"You're dripping on the rug," Pamela said, looking up from her magazine. Pamela is our receptionist. I felt she wasn't showing proper sympathy to her lord and master.

"It's raining."

She shifted in her seat and gave me a stern stare.

"I know," she said. "Will you expect me to dry the rug?"

I ignored her. She opened her desk drawer, reached in and handed me a paper towel.

I took the towel and started to rub my hair and face. The paper became so soaked, it started to fall apart. Pamela handed me another one, without comment. I didn't know how long this was going to go on. On the other hand, I didn't intend to find out.

"Clyde," I called out.

"In my office, Jimmy." His voice was muted by the closed door.

Actually, Clyde's office was my office until we made Clyde a partner. Since he does most of the legal work, Karen told me he needed an office. I didn't mope or make a scene. I've found that doesn't work out so well when Karen makes a decision. Now I use the conference room.

The conference room used to be the library before books became obsolete. Karen let me have a computer. I actually use it when I figure out how to turn it on.

Sure enough, Clyde was in his office typing on his laptop. His face had a look of concentration.

His office was the small downstairs bedroom before our house became our office. It's about 15 by 15. It has a plaster ceiling with figures molded into it. Real old school workmanship. Karen painted it blue.

There is a window that looks out over the marina. I used to watch pretty topless girls on the boats anchored there. That was before it started raining. I don't think Clyde cared. I missed the view.

"One second, Jimmy. I don't want to lose this phrase," Clyde said continuing to work at his computer without looking up.

I took one of the client's chairs across from Clyde. I made squishing sounds and continued to rub at myself with the paper towel.

Clyde was dressed in a dark brown cashmere cardigan with leather buttons. He had it buttoned up almost to the neck. His tan cashmere rolled top shirt showed above the collar of the cardigan. He was well turned out. I'm sure he got that from me. Probably hero worship.

He is a handsome black man, a little over 6 feet tall. His skin tone is light and the only fault was his nose which must have been broken at some time and poorly reset. It makes him look interesting. He is trim, fit and athletic. I could hate him if I didn't like him so much.

He looked warm. I wasn't. Being wet from head to toe is not inducive to a warm personality. I gave a little shiver.

There was a cup of steaming coffee on Clyde's desk. He pushed it towards me as he looked up and smiled. I gripped it with both hands and let the steam warm my face. I sighed.

"You be dripping on my rug, Boss," Clyde said, pointing his index finger at me. Clyde plays with dialect. He thinks it's funny.

I ignored that and leaned towards Clyde. The leather squeaked beneath me as I moved. A rivulet of water leaked on the seat cushion and ran over the front of the chair, dripping onto the toe of my shoe. I reached down with the paper towel to dry my shoe and got another rivulet of water over my hand. This paper towel was falling apart too.

"I just came from Sal's," I said giving up and sitting up straight. I bear up well under adversity. I've had a lot of training.

"Nice haircut. What's that cut on your cheek?"

"Sal told me that Rusty Krinik died," I said, without responding to Clyde's question.

Just as I was speaking, a gust of wind drove the rain against the window, rattling it noisily.

Clyde leaned towards me. "It's raining so hard I don't think I heard you right. Can you repeat that?"

He pursed his lips and shook his head. His eyes narrowed. "Did you say Rusty Krinik died?"

"Yes." I raised my voice a little. I leaned forward too.

Clyde's mouth turned down. "That's awful. He was a good mayor. And a friend." Clyde kept Rusty as a friend even after we sued the city for damages as a result of my imprisonment. Clyde had a knack for making people like him. Of course, he probably also learned that from me. I mentored Clyde over the years into the terrific lawyer he has become. I'm too modest to take credit.

"Was he sick?" Clyde asked, raising the pen he was holding to rub against his cheek. He did that when he was disturbed.

"Healthy as a horse. He was run over by a steam roller."

The rain continued to cover the windows. I couldn't even see the marina. It looked cold out there.

Clyde cocked an eyebrow and his eyes widened. He put down the pen and settled back into his chair. "Unusual," he said. "Is the town in trouble?"

I went through everything Sal had said.

"Do you know whether there will have to be an election for Rusty's remaining term or will the City Council just name a replacement?" I asked. Blissfully, I had stopped leaking on the chair, although I don't recommend you have an extended conversation in wet pants. It tends to be irritating.

Clyde gave me one of those hands apart, palms up gestures. "Let me look."

He turned back to his computer and did some stuff. He's really good at doing stuff. I have no idea what stuff, but he's good at it. He murmured something I didn't catch, shook his head, read for a while and jotted down some notes. Then he turned in his chair and looked back up at me.

"The City Charter says the Council has the option to appoint an interim person but has to hold an election within 90 days to elect a mayor to fill the remaining term."

"That means the person they appoint as interim mayor will have a really big advantage," I said.

"Nope. The Charter specifies that person can't run."

Clyde paused and turned reflective. He was looking over my shoulder into the distance somewhere. He picked up the ball point pen again and put the end in his mouth and tapped it on his teeth. The end without the ink. Clyde is a smart fellow.

"This new mayor is going to be important," he finally intoned. "There's a lot of development going on up and down the coast. Rusty was always opposed to that kind of thing."

"But the mayor doesn't make that decision."

Clyde shook his head. "No. But he has a lot of influence. And he votes on the City Council."

"I think we're okay then. Our City Council members have always voted to make sure we don't change San Buenasara."

"I sure hope so. I like it here," Clyde said, with a wistful smile that slipped from his face as he continued. "Those development plans those people were pushing last year were awful. A resort hotel and shopping center. It would have ruined the town." He shook his head.

"Yeah, I like it here too."

Clyde paused and put down the pen. He looked at me closely.

"Jimmy, why don't you run?"

"No way. I would be lousy at the job."

"Yeah, you would be," he said slowly, in a reflective way. Hey, where's the respect?

It would be nice to be appreciated.

"But at least we'd know that you wouldn't do anything wrong."

That's funny. I didn't know I wouldn't do anything wrong. I mean, I wouldn't do anything wrong on purpose, but I had, on occasion, zigged when I should have zagged. Actually, on more than one occasion. To tell the truth, quite a lot.

"Clyde, there's no way I am going to run for mayor. I've been involved in two murders." Actually, only one, although I was almost convicted of the second.

"Even in San Buenasara I couldn't be elected," I said with some confidence.

"Maybe not. I'm not so sure. But what about Karen?"

Karen's my past and present wife.

"I think she's getting a real kick out of law school," I said. Karen had decided to go back to school. And she deserved it. It had been a long time in coming. I could sense how excited she was about what she was learning and how stimulated she felt. Her eyes shined and she couldn't wait to tell me about her day. There was no way I was even going to suggest she give that up.

I certainly wasn't about to suggest that Clyde run. I enjoyed having food on the table every night and would like to see that continue. So, I guess we would just wait and see who would be our next mayor.

Chapter 3

I WAS BEAT WHEN we finally got upstairs. Thinking wears me out.
Upstairs is where we live. We have a bedroom and a sitting room.
We installed a bathroom and a tiny kitchen. It works out well.

Suddenly, Karen wanted to have her way with me. I think she
was aroused by my brilliance. It is hell to be so attractive. She
pounced upon me, throwing me on the bed. I bounced, but stead-
ied. She crawled in next to me, laughing, and fingered the buttons
on my shirt. The rain glistening in the windows gave our bedroom
a romantic glow.

I rose to the occasion. Karen noticed. She is very observant. She
stroked the bulge in my pants. I may have whimpered.

I put up a valiant struggle. I'm as brave as a lion. A rather small
one. Okay, I'm a good loser. She pulled down my zipper and gently loosened our mutual friend from his captivity. She gave him a
welcoming kiss.

To tell the truth, I had been nervous when Karen and I married.
Remarried? We had such a great relationship after our accidental
divorce. But we had been divorced and now we were married.
Would our relationship change? Would we become stale? Would
we have sex? None of that had happened. I mean none of that but
the sex. Karen is a great lover. Inspired by me.

As matters progressed, so did I. So, I slept well.

I was yawning as I came down the stairs. It must have been 9 o'clock, practically the middle of the night. Karen had been up and out the door, with Bruno and the Jaguar at 8:30. We had owned the Jaguar for years.

The staircase opens into the reception area for the firm. Pamela, our receptionist was there, a miracle unto itself, and so was a small, chubby man in a really nice suit, smiling up at me. He had dark curly hair and ears that stuck out a little, giving him an impish look. He seemed to be about my age, although it was hard to judge looking down.

I was presentable in my pressed jeans and one of my flannel shirts. My boots were shined.

"Mr. Harris, Mr. Marino is here to see you."

Pamela only calls me Mr. Harris in front of clients. That's good. I just wasn't up to dealing with a bill collector.

I put out my hand and he shook it.

"Hi, I'm Jimmy Harris."

"Ah, Mr. Harris. I am Paolo Marino. From Etaly." He spoke in deeply accented English. I noticed there was a kind of joyful energy around this man. That interested me.

"Mr. Marino, why don't we go into the conference room."

We walked across the small reception area to the door on the far side of Pamela's desk. I opened it and held the door for my potential new client.

"It always rain here so much?" he asked.

"Not really. This is very unusual, Mr. Marino."

"You calla me Paolo. I am not stand on the ceremony."

"Great. And call me Jimmy." Being on a first name basis with a potential client never hurt.

"I see pretty woman leaving as I come here. Have beautiful dog. I have dog in Umbria. I like dogs. I pet him. He shake my hand." That was a good sign. Bruno doesn't shake hands with everyone. Unless, of course, he suspects they have food and will share.

"That was Karen, my wife. Our dog's name is Bruno. I sometimes think she likes him more the she likes me," I said, closing the door of the conference room.

"You funny man, Jemmy," he said shaking his head.

"Won't you have a seat," I said, gesturing to one of the black leather chairs around the conference table. The conference room is painted a simple light yellow. One wall has floor to ceiling shelves filled with law books. They are for show. There is not a lot on the other walls. There is a painting we picked up a few years ago at a garage sale and a couple of posters. It has one window that looks out onto our neighbor's house, although today you could not see a whole lot.

Paolo pulled out a chair next to the end of the table and sat down. I took the seat at the end, next to him.

"May I get you coffee or tea, Paolo?" I was hoping he would ask for tea. Offering Pamela's coffee was always a risk.

"No, no. I am good. I want talk to you." He made a gestured with an open hand. Paolo seemed very gregarious.

It made sense that he wanted to talk to me, since he came to our office.

He leaned forward. I got a whiff of his cologne. Not too heavy. He had good teeth. But his hands look roughened.

"I am chef. You maybe heard of me."

I shook my head sadly. "No, I probably should have, but I don't get out much." I hadn't even heard of Janet Mason, the star of the hit television series *Desperate Shop Girls* and my former, now deceased, client.

"I have great restaurant in Pienza. It have two stars from the Michelin. Very good. You know Pienza? Es beautiful." His eyes were alight with the thought.

"Is that in Italy?" No one ever said I wasn't a master of deduction.

"Yes, Etaly. Very nice. Very rustic. Little village there, on top of hill." He sounded kind of disappointed. I'd have to look it up on a map after he left.

"Great. What can I do for you?"

"I want you, how you say it, represent me. You know, tell me how to do deal."

This was looking up. Paolo had come to the right place.

"How did you find me?"

"You are great avvocato I read about. You represent famoose movie star."

Actually, Janet Mason was a television star. Television, movies, what difference did it make if she was famoose.

"I did represent Janet Mason. It was a quite successful matter."

Well, yes, although I didn't achieve quite the result Janet had hoped for. I guess it depends on how you define successful. I survived. She didn't. That wasn't my fault either.

My thoughts came to an abrupt stop. Wait a minute. Did this guy just call me an avocado. Is he implying I'm some kind of fruit? Or is it a vegetable? I mean, he's insulting me even before he retains me. It usually takes my clients weeks before they start calling me names.

"Avocado?" I gave him a ferocious look which might be interpreted as puzzlement to the less aware.

"No, no. No avocado. Avvocato. It mean attorney in Italian." He made a broad hand gesture that indicated he was concerned.

Oh, then, that was okay. "You said something about a deal, Mr. Marino?"

"No, no. Please. Paolo. We be friends." Paolo opened his arms. I was afraid he was going to stand up and kiss me on both cheeks.

"Wonderful, Paolo." I waited. The rain ran down the window.

"People come to me. Say I can make wonderful restaurant here in San Buenasara." He touched his chest with an open hand for emphasis. "Need great restaurant. They say they represent City. Give me money. I know nothing of these things. So, I come to great avvocato."

Ah, the plot thickens. So, the guys who want to change everything want a high-end restaurant too. Not with my help. I didn't even ask how much money was involved. I was proud. I thought about asking. But I didn't.

"Paolo, I'm sorry. I can't represent you." I took out my handkerchief and blew my nose. "I really like San Buenasara the way it is. It's laid back and unassuming. I think I could have a conflict. I mean, I might have to do something that would not be good for you."

"Jemmy, I no want to change town. One reason I like idea is because town is so good. You know, real place."

That's the first time anyone has called San Buenasara real. It pretty much floats a few feet above real.

"Perfect for my restaurant." Paolo seemed truly concerned that I thought he wanted to change San Buenasara.

"Would not be good for me to be in not pretty town. I help you. You help me. I want what you want. My restaurant be jewel on tattered cushion. Like in Pienza." He lifted his hand with the fingers splayed for emphasis.

Wow, this guy really was Italian. I thought we might be able to put that to music. Hum a few bars.

"Paolo, I should warn you. There is already a great Italian restaurant here."

Mario's is a little Italian restaurant Karen and I like, tucked back from the highway in Arroyo Grande, a few miles down the road. Checkered table cloths and candles dripping from old Chianti bottles. It's cheap, and the food is good.

"You no worry, Jimmy. I eat with Mario already. He come from village near where I come from. I like Mario. Our restaurant not the same. I make good restaurant for you."

"Paolo, we love San Buenasara the way it is. I'm glad you do too. And I think a great restaurant will be a swell addition. If you're sure you're okay with the way it is, then I'm in. If you want, I think I can do what you need," I said rising and extending my hand.

Paolo rose too. "Thank you, Jemmy. We do work together. You good man." Paolo ignored my hand, hugging me and kissing me on both cheeks.

And this good man still had time for breakfast. It was only 9:30. I had to walk to the Lilly Pad, but a little rain never hurt anyone. I was hungry.

Chapter 4

I KNOW I MENTIONED it was raining. But it wasn't just raining. It was one of those rare, back-to-back El Nino years. You know, where the Pacific Ocean rears up and dumps most of itself on our parched, semi-arid plain. Something about warming and ocean currents. I'm not too good at the technical stuff. I am good at knowing I'm all wet, which I try to avoid as much as possible.

And in this unusual instance, the weather people had been right. San Buenasara was floating down an atmospheric river. One storm had been following another like a parade of circus elephants stomping down the road. It had been raining in biblical proportions and I swear my neighbors were building an ark. I hoped they were taking reservations.

Our lakes were overstuffed and San Buenasara Creek, the unassuming stream that separates us peons from the Pointe, was roaring a robust welcome to September.

Whatever warming out in the ocean that was causing all this was noticeably absent in the air today and my nose was red and sore. I was struggling to keep my umbrella right-side in and the rain right-side out. I had been notably unsuccessful.

The rain was turning my neatly pressed blue jeans into clinging tights. No doubt, with my shapely legs, I would look good in tights. But I would prefer to be given the choice.

I would like to make a pun here, but I'm afraid if I opened my mouth my tongue would drown. That wouldn't be good for my career as a great lawyer. So I'll keep my mouth shut. I had looked longingly at my good suede jacket when I dressed this morning. Would I ever wear it again? I love that jacket.

I struggled to the door of the Lilly Pad and opened it to a glorious sense of warmth and the smell of hot cinnamon buns. I shook my umbrella the way a dog shakes himself after running in the ocean. That didn't turn out to be such a good idea. Lilly, my esteemed friend and the owner of the Lilly Pad, happened to be walking by the door and received my offering. Lilly is short, round and vocal. She was not amused based upon the words she muttered that cast doubt on my lineage.

"Oh Lilly, I'm so sorry. I didn't see you there."

Let me tell you, my heart was in it. To be banished from the Lilly Pad was effectively to be excommunicated from the church. The Lilly Pad is the communications center of our little town, at least on an integrated basis. On the basis of sex, you have Sal's. And you have Susie's. But Lilly's can't be beat for range and breadth. And Lilly also has good food.

She glowered at me, but I gave her my patented repentant smile and she softened.

"I'm so sorry," I said again.

"Oh, it's okay, Jimmy. It will save me having to shower tonight." She was only kidding, I think. She turned and went on her way, leaving a trail of wet footprints behind her. I blew my nose.

Lilly feeds me breakfast every morning. Then I power walk back to my office. Even in the rain. I'm a sturdy guy. Yes, the office is downhill, just a few blocks. But downhill after breakfast is good.

The Lilly Pad is the best restaurant in San Buenasara. It has a unique décor. Lilly is a sucker for frogs. I think Lilly spent years and a lot of hard nights trying to find her prince. She must have kissed a lot of them. There were frog murals, frog figurines, even frogs on the cups. The Lilly Pad was painted frog green. She hasn't gotten around to adding frog's legs to the menu yet, thank goodness.

The rains had been a Godsend for the Lilly. It was an advertising coup. And it was free. A cacophony of frog song advertised the Lilly Pad at dusk every night.

Karen and I had our own special booth. The best in the house. It was the one that had not only a view out the front door, but also a partial view of the kitchen. The red vinyl was pristine, except for the one small place that was mended with red tape. You wouldn't notice it unless you looked. And the frog figurines on the edge of the booth were unique. Lilly had brought them back from San Francisco last month. Handmade by some well-known French artist, she said.

Karen had gotten to the Lilly Pad before me. She had an early morning meeting. Something that had to do with a classmate at law school.

"It's raining," she had said when she grabbed the car keys this morning as she was going out the door. I knew that. What I didn't reflect on was my situation. I would have to walk. I mean, uphill. Hey, that wasn't fair. She took advantage of me when I was still sleeping. I usually don't mind Karen taking advantage of me, but it's more fun when I'm awake. My life is beset by problems.

Karen was sitting in our booth, sipping her orange juice. Her meeting had obviously ended and I was lucky she hadn't left yet. Bruno was lying across Karen's toes. I envied him. He looked dry.

I was aware of my mixed emotions. I love sitting with Karen. I love talking to her. I also love bacon and eggs.

"Hi," I said, ignoring the wet footprints that followed me. "What's up?" Then I sneezed.

"Bless you," she said without looking up, but she smiled. I have a very distinctive sneeze. She held out a tissue. I took it and sat down, grabbing a menu.

I ordered poached eggs with dry toast. I hate dry toast. However, Karen has not been pleased with the weight I've gained. In my view, winter was coming and I needed some more insulation.

I personally think a little heft looks good on a man. Karen agrees. Our only argument we have is over the term "little." Hey, I'm the lawyer. You think I would win that argument. If so, you don't know Karen.

Chapter 5

I'VE MENTIONED KAREN WAS my ex-wife. And my present wife. We remarried last year.

Karen and I have a great relationship. We've always lived together, even after the divorce. She has a pretty, pixyish face. Gamine cut red hair. A light dusting of freckles across her nose that are a little darker under her eyes. Big green eyes. Not hazel. Green with gold specks. The splash of freckles makes them look bigger.

Karen weighs 110 pounds, so she has to watch her weight. She's about my height although she still looks up to me. Her willowy body had great ups and downs and ins and outs. And she has wonderful small breasts. Thank God I opted for the fully equipped model.

There is a deep sensuality about her. She is a woman made for a rumpled bed.

She just didn't want to get married again. She didn't want to get divorced either. After we'd been married for eight years, I fell off the wagon. Hey, it was a bumpy road, and I was under a lot of pressure. But Karen is a zero-tolerance kind of lady. No enabling. Those were the rules.

So, she gave me a chance to get sober while she got a lawyer up in San Luis Obispo and filed for legal separation. This jerk couldn't even check the right boxes. It's a printed form for God's sake. He checked the box for divorce, not legal separation.

I moved out and when I got hold of myself, I moved back in.

Karen asked for a set of the legal papers a year later. She's like that. Thorough. Right on top of the stack of papers in the file was the final divorce decree. We had a good laugh over a glass of white wine. Hers, not mine. I drink non-alcoholic beer. Then she got this look in her eyes.

After the divorce, I proposed to Karen at least 15 times. At least I think it was 15 times. I'm not so good at counting when I run out of fingers. I think taking off your shoes and socks in public is gauche.

When I asked, she'd smile and kiss me. Sometimes she'd drag me off to the bedroom. But she never said "Yes." Last year, she did. No one was more surprised than I was.

We've been in San Buenasera for nine years now. We moved up from L.A. after I had the go around with the State Bar. Mid-life crisis. It really wasn't that serious. And, I've been on the wagon for the last seven years. Almost.

Before we moved, I had a practice in Los Angeles. I did criminal law, which meant I represented a lot of drug dealers. There was stress in my practice. Besides the scum who were my clients, a lot of my stress was created by my erstwhile partner, McNulty.

Things weren't going so hot and McNulty wasn't an honest lawyer. McNulty caused me some wee problems with the Bar.

That's when Karen suggested we move someplace less stressful. Maybe she did a wee bit more than suggest it. I've had many arguments with Karen over the years and I'm proud to say I've almost always had the last word. It's usually "Yes, dear." She has a strong personality.

I'm 47 and I still have the body God gave me. Well, actually that body departed about four years ago and I have the body I suppose I deserve. I like to think my boyish, lopsided grin and my blond hair makes up for it. Oh, and my baby blue eyes. I'm 5'7". At least I was when I was 30. I think I'm shrinking. Unfortunately, not in the waist.

The door to Lilly's opened, letting in a shiver of breeze and Polly breezed in on it. We waved him over and I scooted aside and patted the booth beside me. I hope he didn't notice the seat was wet. I knew something was wrong right away. I am a master of close observation. That was when my red nose first started twitching.

Polly's real name is Randy Polivnacov, but everyone calls him Polly. He's a good guy, very quiet and mellow. Probably because of the uncontrolled substance he favors. Polly never curses or loses his temper.

Now he was furious. I knew this because the tips of his ears had turned red. And he raised his voice and said, "Darn it." Then he pursed his lips and glared. A raindrop fell from his earlobe onto the table. He smelled of wet wool.

When Polly is upset, I listen. He is a pillar of our little community. He's our local pornographer and also one of our longest-serving City Council members. Polly owns the adult toy store. Pussy Galore has the best windows in San Buenasara.

Karen patted Polly's hand. "What's wrong, Polly?"

"That damned cop."

"Which one?"

"Walter Carsone."

"Why?" I asked.

"He's running for mayor," Polly said with a dour look. Polly didn't like Carsone. Carsone had not been one of Polly's admirers either.

"He says he's going to make San Buenasara safe and prosperous."

San Buenasara is not exactly crime ridden. If you exclude all the deaths I've been involved with, it is as safe as a church.

"That sounds kind of good," I said. "Except, maybe the more policing part." In truth, I was being the devil's advocate. I wanted to encourage Polly to tell all.

"That's part of the problem, Jimmy," Polly said a little petulantly. Apparently, Polly does not like having his chain tugged.

"I don't understand," I said. People who know me know that isn't unusual.

At that moment, Lilly wandered by, her arms stacked with plates.

"Don't worry, I hear Carsone will have competition," she said. Obviously, she had overheard Polly talking so loudly. She would never eavesdrop. All of our heads swiveled towards her.

Everyone always seems to know more than I do.

"Who?" Karen asked.

"Susie told me this morning, when I was having my hair done. Allie Niddle says she's going to run. I also hear that Ben may throw his hat in the ring." She shrugged the plates that ran up her arm back into a better position as she talked. How she can stand there and talk with all that weight on her arms astounds me. Note to self. Do not get into a fight with Lilly.

That left us with our mouths gaping open. Okay, Allie Niddle makes sense. But Ben? Ben's our only homeless person.

Lilly wandered away to deliver the goods.

"But Carsone's running for mayor isn't the worst of it," Polly said, ignoring Carsone's new found competition and returning to his own troubles.

"Why not?" Karen asked.

"My landlord says Carsone wants to buy our building."

"So?"

"He doesn't have any money."

"That's going to make it difficult."

"I heard he wants to tear it down and build an upscale shopping center."

"That sounds kind of nice." I said it in jest, but this was serious.

"I think there's a lot of outside money in his campaign. I hear that there are going to be people running for City Council that will be well funded too. Peter Lessing has announced he's running against me."

Ah, the crux of Polly's displeasure. Lessing is a local wealth manager, cum stock broker.

"What do you know about Lessing?" I asked.

"I don't know anything. He just appeared one day a couple of years ago, as far as I know. I don't need much 'wealth management.'"

Neither did I.

"No one ever runs for City Council. I'm scared," Polly said.

"Where are you hearing all this."

"Sal told me." Sal is always right.

"Polly, having some upscale stores wouldn't be so bad, would it?"

"Jimmy, you must be kidding. You don't think it will stop there, do you? Don't get me started."

We already had.

"What happens to me?" Polly said in a stressed voice. "And to you. To the town. You think they want to let us be? No way. They want to turn the town into a fancy place. And they'll want me out."

Polly was getting really excited. For Polly, that meant sitting up straight and focusing his eyes. He was scaring me.

I'm just a poor dirt farmer scratching a living out of the dustbowl of life. But it was this dustbowl I cared about. If Carsone won, things were going to change. And not for the better if the money Polly spoke about was really involved. I was pretty sure Carsone's moral compass had rusted out a long time ago from lack of maintenance.

"Polly, you don't know that." I said it with a touch of concern threaded with hope.

"Yes I do. You know Carsone already wants me out. Jimmy, I provide a good service." Polly said that with the sense of importance of a man close to the heart of the community. "It's only my loyal customers that keep me in business." Polly has influential customers like the Superintendent of Schools and several of our local clergy. Very progressive fellows, our local clergymen.

Polly was right. Once our little town was developed, no one could change it back. It would be gone forever.

Bruno, who had been sleeping on Karen's toes, raised his head and growled. That dog is opinionated, but thoughtful.

Bruno loves San Buenasara the way it is. And he's quite popular. After all, the local dog park is named after him.

He is a long-haired dachshund. Dachshunds are special dogs. They were bred to hunt badgers. And Bruno is a tenacious hunter. He has classic paddle-shaped front paws at the end of his short legs. His long body is tipped by a long snout. He prides himself on his sleek long red coat with brown accents. He's brave. You'd have to be to stick your nose in a badger hole. He is beautiful, and he knows it.

I used to have hair too. I know how he feels.

Chief Carsone had proposed lowering taxes, cutting costs and improving city services. That was a platform I could get behind. Which really scared me senseless. Chief Carsone failed to mention how he intended to pay for that neat little feat.

Since I didn't think he could select his uniform in the morning without assistance, I suspected that others were involved. And if there were others involved, they were outsiders. And that was going to be a problem. Walter Carsone was a man of some stature. He wasn't the kind of man who could be bought. But he could be rented, at a reasonable rate. The question was, who was doing the renting and what did they want.

No one in San Buenasara likes Chief Carsone. His wife included. He was the most unlikely mayoral candidate I could imagine. Until Ben threw his hat into the ring.

There was a problem with Ben's throwing his hat into the ring. Ben doesn't own a hat.

But after all, Allie Niddle was running and she would trounce Carsone.

Chapter 6

WE SPENT SOME TIME calming Polly down. When he finally seemed calm enough, we left. Polly was nursing his coffee and still muttering to himself. We were concerned about leaving Polly alone, but we had taken the knives off the table.

Karen gestured towards the Jaguar which I took to mean I was to be honored with a ride back to our house. I loved that car. It aged beautifully, just like me. At least from the outside. We have a lot in common. It works about 50% of the time. So did I.

It had stopped raining and the ocean glistened, throwing off flashes like diamonds in a shifting light. I thought the sun looked a little abashed, being caught out naked without its blanket of clouds. But it was probably my imagination.

A little breeze made the puddles of water in the street ripple. It was about 60 degrees. Another average day in paradise. My furled umbrella was still dripping on my blue jeans.

Bruno sat in the back seat with his paws on the open window sill. He likes to be chauffeured. He had his head out the window with the wind in his ears. Bruno objects to wet umbrellas, which is why mine was between my legs in front.

The house, which is also our office, is five blocks downhill from Lilly's and a block over towards the water. I was still proud of my walk to the Lilly Pad. I love the exercise. It was only a few blocks sure, but it was uphill, and I still viewed it with pride.

Our little town has maybe seven thousand people on a good day. It's a funky little place.

In what we like to call the Mission District, we have our famous oak tree. According to the Chamber of Commerce, the oak tree was planted by Junipero Serra on his way through town. Everyone else got a mission. We got the tree.

The modern town, if that's the right word, was founded by Spiritualists around the turn of the century. Spiritualism was big then. A lot of people believed that you could talk to the dead through a spiritual medium. Not nutty people. Arthur Conan Doyle was a believer. I guess a lot people wanted to complain to their mother.

The Spiritualists divided up the town into 50-foot lots that they sold to true believers. The true believers arrived on a train that ran through town. It still does, rumbling through twice a day. The believers built little wooden houses, one of which Karen and I live and work in.

During the '60's the town changed with the influx of young folks looking for freedom and love. San Buenasara became notorious for its bellbottoms and hot tubs. Free love tended to make the town mellow, along with the smell of weed that wafted over the entire place.

It has calmed down a bit, although there are more than a few old hippies around. The town still smells of weed, but now it's legal. Actually, you can probably get high by sniffing the air. That may be why it's so laid back.

San Buenasara is a friendly place. We have been spared the developers for the most part, since the debacle at Franklin Farms. Or rather when I created the debacle at Franklin Farms. I still have the scars.

Franklin Farms was the 1,400-acre development of high-end homes undertaken by Guy Mason, Janet Mason's husband. Janet Mason was the client, for whom I am famous. Janet hired me to get her a divorce. She came all the way to San Buenasara to retain me instead of an inferior lawyer in Los Angeles.

Unfortunately, the development was financed by dirty union

money represented by Gino Bartoletti, Janet's boyfriend. Guy Mason had the misfortune to die in a car crash. A small matter of the brake lines being cut. Janet Mason ended up drowning in her pool and I had the unpleasant task of being the one to find her.

Gino Bartoletti was the only one who came out ahead. For just a little testimony against some of his riper colleagues, he received immunity from minor crimes like murder, a new identity and a pension from our federal overseers. Franklin Farms is now a wildlife preserve, except for the 50 acres that comprise the Bruno Harris Dog Park. Bruno is quite proud of it. So are we.

The railroad tracks run between the highway and our little town, so we are on the wrong side of the tracks. Which on the coast is the right side of the tracks. Never mind, its complicated.

For years we rented the house. It's a little, frame, two-story house painted a pretty pastel yellow. There is a tiny lawn and a white picket fence in front. Karen has planted white roses against it. They are bare now.

We bought the house last year during a brief period when we were flush. That hadn't lasted long. Business has been dreadful except for our contract with the city. Even that had been slow. But we're a block from the ocean, with a view.

Karen turned to me.

"Do you think Polly is right?" she asked. There was a concerned look on her face. Her jaw was fixed and the edges of her lips turned down.

"About what Carsone is up to?"

"Yes."

"It makes sense."

"I like our town like it is."

"Me too."

"What do we do?" Karen said.

"No idea. You?"

"None."

"How about you, Bruno. Any thoughts?" Karen asked, looking over at him between the seats. I was glad, at least, she asked me first. Bruno was concentrating on his ears. He kept his own counsel. I was relieved he didn't have a better idea.

"We should sleep on it tonight," I said. Plan ahead.

"You get the wet spot," Karen said. She always has a better plan.

"Can we negotiate?"

"Nope."

She also is always right.

"Maybe Clyde can think of something." I added.

I'm not brilliant. (Well, there are those who would disagree with that, and I guess they could be right.) But I do have a nose for trouble. I had a cold, but I could smell it. I just didn't know yet how bad the smell was going to be.

We made it to the office. I know it is only six blocks but between the Jaguar and Karen's driving, that was an accomplishment.

The Jaguar had had many challenges since I bought it, used, at one of those few minutes that we were flush. It had been my fateful companion during the scary time when Janet Mason was murdered. And it even stood by me when I was in jail for Wee Willy's murder. As to Karen's driving, I will remain prudently silent. Karen parked in our driveway.

"Have you got the time to come in. I think we should speak to Clyde."

Karen looked at her watch and narrowed her eyes. "Maybe 15 minutes."

"Great." I got out of the car and went around to open her door.

"Thank you," she said with a smile. "You are becoming quite the gentleman. I expect you'll want to get laid soon."

Hope springs eternal.

We trooped in. Pamela was apparently on one of her many breaks, so we knocked on Clyde's door and walked in without waiting.

He was on the telephone finishing a call. His desk looked like it had been caught in a violent wind storm. Carl Jung said a messy desk is the mark of a great mind. Clyde could be his poster boy today.

We sat down in the clients' chairs across from him. To his credit, he wasn't looking out the window at the marina. I had spent a lot of my time looking out that window before I chose to move to the conference room. I missed the view. I always found it uplifting.

Karen is still office manager even though she now has law school to add to her duties. Somehow, she gets it all done. She rules with an iron hand. To be totally honest, she rules with other parts too, but that's private.

Clyde has been part of our life for years. He was the son of our one-day-a week cleaning lady, when we could afford one, many years ago. That's how we met him. She was a good Jamaican lady, and sometimes brought him along with her when she came in. He would follow Karen around the office and ask questions. Bright kid.

His mother died suddenly when Clyde was about 15. We took Clyde in to live with us for a few days until we could sort things out. He only moved out about a year ago.

We knew Clyde was smart, although, honestly, we didn't know how smart. Or, at least I didn't. He needed something to do after school, so we started letting him help us around the law firm. He was really good. He was curious about everything. And he followed through. Karen kept giving him more difficult tasks and monitored how he did.

When he was 20, we talked him into going to law school at night up in San Luis. He didn't want to. He had only graduated high school. But the law school lets you in if you got a good score on the LSAT exam. Clyde got a great score.

He reluctantly agreed to give it a try. He finished first in his class with the best grades they ever recorded, although that record may be in jeopardy now that Karen is there.

We paid for all of Clyde's schooling. It sounds magnanimous, and I guess in a sense it was. But it was the best money we ever spent. Clyde came to work for us. He is one heck of a lawyer.

Last year we made him a partner. Karen told me we had to be-cause he was doing all the work. I thought that was grossly unfair. What about experience and style.

I did it anyway. I always do what Karen tells me. "Yes, Dear" has been a sound response for me most of my life with Karen. Unless

I feel compelled to say, "Of course, Dear."

I even let Clyde pay out his partnership buy-in. He called it his pay cut. That was ungrateful. In truth, I wouldn't know what we would do without him. Probably close up the shop. When he almost left us last year for a big job in Los Angeles, that is what we thought of doing.

"Hey, Clyde," I said.

"Yo, Boss," he nodded at me. "Boss lady."

Clyde thinks playing the black man is funny. It might be if I didn't know he could speak better English than I can and probably has a better vocabulary. Strike "probably."

"A problem has come to pass," I said.

"You mean the one where our town is destroyed and we are tarred and feathered and driven into the wilderness attached to a stake."

"Right, that one," I said. "You heard."

"Yeah, I did." He opened his hands. "So?"

I explained to Clyde what Polly had told us.

"That figures," he said after I finished.

"How so?" I asked.

"I just got a call from Sarah." Sarah was the nurse Clyde has been dating for the last year. Smart girl, pretty.

"She just got an eviction notice. Some big company bought up the entire apartment complex she lives in." Clyde tipped back in his office chair with a squeak.

"The big one out by the school?" I asked.

He tipped his chin forward. "That one."

"Why did they evict her?"

"They evicted everybody. All 200 folks. Gave them 30 days. Said they going to build luxury apartments and condos. Seems like someone's putting in a lot of money around here all of a sudden."

"We like San Buenasara like it is," Karen said.

"Me too. Don't want a lot of them rich honkeys pollutin' things." Clyde can be as down home as corn pone in Alabama.

"Clyde, you should wash out your mouth with soap," I said. We have standards. Admittedly, not many.

"Sho enough, Boss," he said with a smile. "What we gonn'a do about it?"

"We were hoping you might have an idea."

"Umm," he said, pursing his lips. "I might at that. Let me think about it."

Chapter 7

"WE NEED TO FIGURE out how to help Polly get re-elected," I said.

"And help us," Karen added.

Karen and I were walking back to the office from the Lilly Pad the next day. She had the day off from school. It was sunny in a cloudy kind of way. The sun and clouds made shadows play and slip along the street. There was a breeze blowing off the ocean and it was pleasant for a change. But the clouds were bruised, threatening more rain.

"That may not be so easy, Jimmy. We can figure on whoever is financing Carsone and Polly's opponent buying up all the news, radio and TV. This is a small town and the advertising won't cost that much. If they really are looking to develop San Buenasara, we will be small change to them."

Bruno was trotting along behind us, taking in the rays. He seemed oblivious to our concerns. He is always oblivious to mine.

"Polly has a lot of friends," I said.

"He has real name recognition."

"Who is this guy running against him?" I asked.

"I don't know him," Karen responded. "At least I don't know a lot. I've nodded to him a few times, but we've never had a real conversation." Karen was wearing jeans and a yellow wool sweater, carrying an umbrella. She's smarter than I am.

"Pretty much the same with me. How is that possible? This

town only has 7,000 people."

"Maybe he just came to town," Karen said. I guess she hadn't heard my conversation with Polly.

We were making great time downhill. Walking with Karen was always a treat.

"Polly said he's been here for a couple of years."

"How is he running if no one knows him?"

"I think Polly has the votes," I said it with more hope than fervor.

"I agree."

"The problem is making sure the voters are not all stoned on voting day." People have always been awed by my perspicacity, although that thought didn't take great insight, given our long experience with the citizens of San Buenasara.

"So, for the moment," Karen said, "I think we need to focus on the mayor's race."

Karen turned and looked up at me for my concurrence. I know that we're the same height, but I could feel her looking up.

"I agree. It comes first. The mayor could be the swing vote on the City Council. At least we have some candidates. Allie's a first-class lady," I said.

"But what about Ben? If he runs, he could syphon votes away from Allie. Ben's not be the ideal candidate, any way you look at it."

"No, he isn't. Do you think we can get him to drop out?" I asked sagely.

Karen reached over and took my hand.

"Maybe. But let's wait and make sure Allie is in the race," she said. "Ben may be our only alternative."

"God help us all," I said, looking up to the sky.

"We need to know who he is?" she continued. "I mean what's his history. I don't know anything about him." Karen's cheeks were flushed by the cool breeze. Her face was serious.

"I don't think anyone does. He just moved into his tent one day and has been here ever since."

"He doesn't make trouble. He just goes about his business, whatever that is." Karen's voice echoed the question in her words.

"I like him, but I never thought much about Ben. I have no idea what he believes. It can't be worse than Carsone, anyway"

"He came here how long ago?" Karen asked.

"I think it was about three years. One morning there was a tent in front of City Hall. There was Ben."

"I remember the fuss. It was hilarious."

"Half the City Council wanted to get the police to tear down the tent and evict him. The other half pretty much were hazy about the problem and thought the tent looked kind of neat. So, it stayed, with Ben inside."

"I never met him for at least the first 6 months."

"Neither did I. I saw him around town every now and then. But he and I never really talked."

I nearly tripped over a crack in the pavement. The infrastructure of San Buenasara, if I can use so grandiose a term, was falling to pieces and had been for two decades. Karen put her hand on my arm and I caught myself before I landed on my face. I grumbled some oaths. I think I said "golly." I may even have said "darn." Then I finished my thought.

"Ben seems like an okay guy if we really want him to run. He doesn't look too bad. He would be presentable if he had a shave and a shower. Maybe some decent clothes. But, I don't even know if he can read, much less what he believes."

"We don't have any idea whether he can give a speech."

"We can get someone to help him if it comes to that."

"I guess," I said.

"Does he have any friends?"

"Not that I know of." I was watching my feet now. I almost didn't see the lamppost. I jinked left at the last minute. You have to be athletic to walk the streets of San Buenasara. Bruno yipped and jumped back. That boy can move fast when he wants to. He barked his disapproval. "Sorry, guy," I said, turning my face to him.

Karen gave me a funny look, but I ignored it. I needed to focus on my analysis of our possible candidate.

"Ben's pretty much of a loner, as far as I know. Stays in his tent most of the time. Some folks bring him food. He washes up at City Hall in the public bathroom. At least when he washes up. That's what Lilly told me."

We were quiet for a minute, both thinking about Ben.

Karen broke the silence. "We'll have to do a background check on Ben before we consider helping him. I kind of hope we don't have to. A pretty deep check. I'm sure the Carsone people will, if he runs. I'll ask Clyde how to do that."

"I'm pretty sure we'll have some interesting questions about old Ben," I added. "Frankly, I'm glad Allie's in the race. Ben may have a lot of issues."

"Issues like who would vote for him," Karen said.

"I would vote for him. Anyone would be better than Carsone. Even Bruno."

Bruno perked up at the mention of his name. Maybe there was food involved.

We turned into the door to the office.

Chapter 8

ALLIE NIDDLE, OUR NEW candidate for mayor, was the school counselor and a very smart lady. And best of all, she was a cool woman who had been in San Buenasara her whole life.

Her father and mother were the children of one of the Spiritualist families that settled the town originally and some said that Allie had been a kind of wild child when the town had given itself over to the hippies. She grew up and went away to school.

She had returned to San Buenasara after she got her Master's Degree at UCLA. That says something. The town does not have a lot of boosters. It lacks culture and a place to get a good bagel.

I ran into Allie later that day, outside the local grocery store. Karen sent me out to buy milk. I enjoy shopping for groceries. It feels comforting being around all that food.

I didn't go to the big store up the 101. I like it better when I can go to Harry's, the little corner store off Main Street. Harry is a good guy and can squeeze a tomato with the best of them.

Allie was standing to the side of Harry's front doors. She had her back turned to me and was looking down at the screen of her phone. I touched her arm. She jumped and muffled a scream. I jumped too. Allie almost dropped the phone.

Allie is a small, trim woman, attractive for someone in their late 50s. She was carrying an umbrella, a wise precaution these days.

"Allie, I'm sorry I startled you."

"Oh, Jimmy, it's you" She seemed visibly relieved. She managed a small smile. "Forgive me. I've had a terrible morning."

"Karen and I are really pleased that you're running for mayor. What can we do to help?"

"Do you guys offer armed security?" She said it with a tight mouth.

To say the least, it was not the response I expected.

"What?"

"Because of the guy who was sitting on the fender of my car when I came out of City Hall"

"Huh?" I'm the soul of articulation. I reached up and rubbed the side of my nose. I avoided the part that was sore. My nose had been running and all the blowing had made it sore and red at the tip. This cold was annoying.

"Yes. Have you ever had an ugly man sitting on the fender of your car, looking straight at you. I mean, if you are a woman."

Even if you're a man.

"That was after you had been talking about running for mayor."

"Oh, I was going to run. I could have won. No one likes Carsone. That's why I was at City Hall. I was getting my papers. You know. Finding out the process. What I had to do. I spent some time catching up with friends. I must have been in there for half an hour."

"You were willing to give up your school job to be mayor?"

"That was hard. I love what I do. I could still work part time, but it was still hard. I thought I could be a good mayor. I care about this town. Now, I'm not going to run."

"You'd make a great mayor. Why won't you run?"

"Because I'm scared, Jimmy. I never thought I would be scared in my own town." There was a noticeable tremble in her voice. Her eyes looked frightened and that frightened me.

"What happened?"

"When I came out of City Hall there he was, sitting on the front fender of my car." She was shifting nervously on her feet.

"How could he know you were at City Hall?"

"That's the frightening thing. He must have been following

me." Now she was clearly upset. Her hands were trembling. She clamped them together to try to still them.

"Do you think he knows where you live?"

"I know he does. He told me what a nice little house I have, but that I needed to get the fence fixed." She looked in jerky movements over her shoulders at the people around her.

"I asked him what he meant. He said it was damaged. When I got home, several of the pickets had been broken. Kicked completely in."

"Did you recognize him."

"I've never seen him before in my life. And I never want to see him again."

"What did he look like?"

"He was short and square. At least I think he was short. Very intimidating. And really ugly."

"What did this guy say to you?" I asked.

"He tried to sound pleasant. He spoke very quietly. He said terrible things in the most ordinary way. It was more threatening than anything."

"What exactly did he say?"

"He told me how Chief Carsone would make a great mayor." She laughed in an unlaughing way.

I nodded.

"He said maybe I should consider whether I wanted to confuse people." Allie was on the verge of tears.

"Confuse?"

"He said politics was ugly and I seemed like a nice lady. Nice ladies don't get involved in ugly things."

"What did you think he meant?"

"I didn't have to think about it. He told me."

"What?" I asked it too quickly. This was scaring me too.

"He said that there had been incidents of houses burning down with people in them."

I knew about that one from experience.

"He told me people had been run over. Hurt."

"Just like Rusty, our former mayor."

"He said people even had gotten killed. Whole families."

"What did you do?"

"I stood there with my mouth open. I was so scared I couldn't move. He hopped off the fender of my car and smiled at me. He actually smiled. You don't want anyone ever to smile at you like that. He said, 'You seem like a good lady. I wouldn't want to see you have trouble. You do the right thing.'"

The right thing being to go home, shut up and not run for mayor.

"Then he said, 'See you around.' He patted my arm and walked away."

"Did you report this to the police?"

"Jimmy, Carsone is running for mayor."

"So, you're not running."

"Absolutely not. I'm scared shitless."

I had never heard Allie swear.

Chapter 9

THE NEXT MORNING AT the Lilly Pad I told Karen that Allie had decided not to run. Before I could get into a lot of details, Lilly distracted us with the news that Ben had announced his candidacy. The sun was making a valiant effort to hold off the rain although it seemed to be fighting a losing battle.

Clyde was in the reception room pouring himself a cup of coffee and chatting with Pamela when we walked in. Both are acts only a stout-hearted fellow like Clyde would undertake. The room smelled of burnt coffee.

Pamela's coffee is in great demand over in the marina. It's used to sear barnacles from the bottom of boats. She once thought about selling it, but it ate through the containers before she could ship them.

He looked up as we came in.

"Hey, Karen. Hi there, Bossman."

"Clyde, I told you not to call me Boss."

"Why Mr. Harris, I'm not calling you 'Boss.' I'm calling you 'Bossman.' That's completely different." Clyde thinks he's being funny.

A big smile broke across his face. Clyde has very white, straight teeth. That orthodontist we paid had done well by doing good.

I threw up my hands. Karen just laughed. I think she thinks Clyde is funnier than I am. That's impossible, right?

"Clyde, have you been thinking about our problem?" Karen said.

He smiled a smile at Karen that crinkled his eyes.

"Absolutely," he said, giving her a bow and a sweeping hand gesture. "Please come into my office here."

We trooped in. The clouds were playing with the light streaming in the window. The marina looked cold. No one was out on the deck of any of the boats. There were certainly no topless women. Good. I could concentrate.

We took seats across from him.

"Yeah, so we got Carsone running for mayor," Clyde started.

"And someone's running against Polly for the City Council."

Clyde shook his head. "That doesn't sound good either."

"Do you think our first priority should be to figure out how to help Polly?" I said. I was taking the bull by the horns, the tiller in my hand. After all, I am the senior partner.

"What about the mayoral election," Clyde asked.

"I don't think that's as pressing a problem, even though Allie isn't running," I said with some authority.

"Allie's not running?" Clyde said.

"No, she got warned off. But there's a candidate who's already running against Carsone and Carsone's not very popular. I mentioned it to you yesterday, Clyde."

"You said something about Ben," Clyde said.

"He's announced now. We heard it at the Lilly Pad when we were having breakfast."

"Announced?"

"Yeah, he told Sal he's running."

"The homeless guy?" Clyde said it reflectingly. He was tapping his fingers on the desk.

I leaned forward in my chair. "Yeah, the guy who lives in the tent by City Hall."

"Do you think Ben can beat Carsone?" Karen asked, turning towards me.

"Maybe. I think the Aflac Duck could beat Walter Carsone."

Clyde put his knuckle to his lip and leaned back. His eyes were quiet and he seemed to turn inward for a few seconds.

I was watching him. Karen, of course, was watching me.

"Clyde, is there a problem?" I asked.

Clyde came back upright in his chair. "I don't know, Jimmy. There might be. Give me a few minutes to look at some books."

"Sure." Clyde was much better at looking at books than I was. Of course, he wasn't looking at books. He was looking at his computer.

Karen and I got up and went out to see what mail Pamela had for us. She handed us a stack of mail and some call slips.

We still have hard telephone lines into the office. I think having an office number and a receptionist gives us some class. I also don't like answering the phone myself. I think it goes back to when I was representing a lot of drug dealers. There are people you do not want to talk to. Believe me. You do not.

We walked into the conference room and put the mail down on the table. We busied ourselves for the next few minutes looking through the mail. I was starting to sweat.

It was becoming uncomfortably warm and humid in our offices. One of the downsides of not having air conditioning. No one does in our little town. We would only need it a few days a year, and it's expensive. My shirt was starting to stick to my side. I tugged at it. It didn't help.

"Boy, it's getting clammy," I said to Karen.

"I noticed," she responded. She's much more heat tolerant than I am. At that point, our discussion abruptly ended.

"Guys," Clyde called out.

Karen and I got up. Being the gentleman that I am, I made a hand gesture to have her precede me through our little reception area into Clyde's office. I noticed Pamela was on one of her breaks. I thought fleetingly about where she was and whether she worked more at her breaks than she did at her job. I discarded the thought as hopeless.

Clyde's door was open. When we entered, he was frowning and shaking his head.

"What?"

"I was afraid of this?"

"Of what?" asked Karen.

"I looked at the municipal code. Section 476 (c). It defines who can run for city office."

"What's the problem?" I asked, somewhat nervously.

"It says that to run, you have to have a permanent residence in the city."

"Ben has been here for three years."

"A tent isn't considered a permanent residence. The code provides that you have to have an address. He's going to get thrown out. Is there another candidate."

"No. Not now."

"Do you think we can get one?"

"We can try, but I don't think so," said Karen. "It's a crappy job."

"Karen, maybe you should run."

"Not me, I've got my hands full with law school. It's important to me."

"Sure, I understand that." Clyde turned towards me. "I already talked to Jimmy," he said, dismissing me from consideration. I was pleased there was no one else in the room.

"I'm probably the only person who can't beat Carsone," I said.

"Jimmy," Karen said. "No one blames you for Janet Mason's death. And everyone knows you were innocent, even though they had you in jail for Willy's murder."

"Maybe," I replied. "But I don't think it's smart for us to try to find out."

"I agree," said Clyde. "It would be a bad idea."

"Damn it," I said, "this town is really going to the dogs."

Karen sat up straight. "That's brilliant," she said.

I knew that.

"Huh," I professed with remarkable insight.

"We'll run Bruno!" Karen said with real excitement, almost delight. She clapped her hands. When Karen smiles, she lights up the room. And she was really smiling.

"You think a dog can beat Carsone?"

"Of course not. But we will embarrass him so much, someone

else will step up. It will be a great joke."

"Karen, that's not a bad idea," said Clyde. "Everyone loves Bruno. We'll use what Jimmy said as his campaign tagline."

"What did I say?"

"San Buensara is going to the dogs!" Clyde announced, with his hands outstretched.

"Maybe, even, 'Don't keep this woof from your door.'"

"I like it," said Karen, laughing.

"How about T-shirts that have a picture of Bruno on the front. And on the back it maybe can say 'Don't Bark Up the Wrong Tree.'" I was getting into this. It was going to be hilarious. We were getting into a giddy mood.

"That one will drive Carsone up the wall." Karen opined.

"It will," I agreed emphatically. After all, it was my idea.

"We should talk about it again tomorrow," Clyde said. "It will be a lot of work."

The rain started to pelt the windows again.

Chapter 10

KAREN, CLYDE AND I were sitting in my office the next morning. We had a dilemma. Actually, a disaster. Yesterday, we had joked about running Bruno. But Karen had picked up on Allie's fear. She's a smart lady. And when she asked, I told her. And she kept asking me questions. We were up half the night. She was upset.

Karen had been through a lot in both the Janet Mason matter and the Wee Willy affair. We had been around people who weren't nice. Very not nice. Frankly they terrified Karen. Fortunately, I was there to protect her. But she was still skittish.

I didn't blame her.

There was a carafe of coffee on the table and some remnants of bagels and a piece of sweet roll. A container of cream cheese was tip to its side, leaning on the knife handle protruding from it.

We'd been at this for 20 minutes. The rain last night had let up, but the windows were still wet. The room seemed warm and muggy. I could feel a bead of sweat run down the inside of my shirt.

"I think we still have to run Bruno," I said, placing my coffee cup firmly on the table.

"Jimmy, I don't want to get involved with people like that again," Karen said. She was dressed in jeans and an old plaid shirt with a frayed collar. She was as beautiful as ever.

"Maybe someone else will file to run. Couldn't we wait before making a decision?" she said.

"I'm willing to wait, but Lilly and Sal don't seem to think anyone else is going to run. We already decided we shouldn't. I've spoken to everyone I know. Clyde, have you heard anything? "

"Nope."

"I just think we have to do something sooner rather than later. We need to shake things up," I said.

"Jimmy, these people scare me." Her eyes were wide and her voice shook a little. She has more sense than I do. As if to make her point, a sharp gust of wind rattled the windows and dark clouds drifted over the sun.

"If we just shake things up, I don't think we'll get involved," I said. "We'll put Bruno's up, make an announcement and then find some reason to withdraw. Carsone will be embarrassed, but if we withdraw, why would he risk making trouble?"

Which shows you how much I know.

"Carsone is a menace," I insisted. "We have to do something. Maybe a joke like this will get some else to run. I just think we have to try. We can't let these people, whoever they are, roll over our town." I was on my high horse. I didn't know you could fall off a high horse. It hurts.

I reached over for the coffee and poured a cup out of the carafe. It was still warm. I knew it was okay to drink. Clyde had a cup and was still alive.

I looked over at him. He just shrugged, pushing the sweet roll on his plate around with his finger. "It doesn't make me happy, Boss. But I sure don't like what's goin' down."

Karen shook her head and got up. "Maybe we have to," she said, obvious reluctance in her voice. She started walking around the room aimlessly. Her lips were pursed and I could hear her uneven breathing. She seemed to have to move.

The lights flicked. We had been having trouble with power outages because of all the wind and rain. It stopped us for a moment, but the lights came back on steadily. We had been thinking about getting a generator for the office. San Buenasara was subject to a lot of power outages, but with everything going on, we hadn't done anything about it.

"Don't we have to file papers?" I said turning to Clyde and putting my cup back on the conference table. Clyde was staring off out the window. "You said that Ben couldn't run because he didn't qualify? How can a dog qualify?"

Karen turned. "Maybe he can't run," she said a little too quickly.

It started raining again, steady, but light. At least it cooled down the conference room. So far, we hadn't had any leaks and the house hadn't washed away. But there was always tomorrow. See, I'm an optimist.

Clyde was dressed in a blue shirt with a Mandarin collar under a dark blue wool blazer with charcoal gray slacks. It's amazing how he always looks so good. If I weren't so pretty myself, I would be jealous.

"That's the good part, Boss. I looked," he said turning to look at me. Karen sat back down, unaccustomedly quiet. She seemed to have closed in on herself. Her hands were in her lap and she had her eyes closed. She raised her hand and started rubbing the bridge of her nose.

"Don't call me 'Boss,'" I said to Clyde rather half-heartedly, for probably the hundredth time.

He ignored me as he always did, and continued.

"The statute requires that to be a candidate for mayor, one must have permanently resided within the city limits of San Buenasara for the preceding three years. It doesn't say anything about being a person."

"You know that's nonsense, don't you. It's clearly implied. It's got to be."

"Boss, I don't write the law. I just follow it."

"Carsone will sue."

"No, he won't." Clyde said it emphatically.

"Why?" I asked in a puzzled voice.

"If he does, he will look like a fool." He tapped his index finger on the table for emphasis. "It will appear he's afraid of running against a dog. That he's so uptight he can't take a joke."

Good point. I had a little bubble of joy rising up inside. I hadn't felt it for a long time. I really didn't like Walter Carsone. The thought of sticking it to him was making me happy.

"Not only would Carsone be mocked," Clyde continued, "a court filing would lead to an explosion of publicity. The newspapers have people monitoring the court filings. I suspect Mr. Carsone and his backers would not want that. People would be taking a much closer look at them. I'll bet they're publicity shy."

"How do we announce this?" I queried.

"Don't know. I've never run a campaign. Do know, if we're going do this, we have to do it right."

"We should do it at the dog park," I suddenly said.

The Bruno Harris Dog Park was a favorite spot in our little town and, as it happens, where Karen and I were married last year.

"Only if it doesn't rain."

"Clyde, that goes without saying. We don't want to drown the voters. That violates some basic rule of politics, I think." I knew that instinctively. I've got great instincts.

"Could be muddy," Clyde said.

I looked out the window. The rain was coming down harder. We'd better also think of some alternative place to have our announcement. But that would have to wait until we got the weather report, for what good that would do us.

"Maybe we can get someone to lay boards. It would be worth it. It's the right place to make the announcement," I finished. I'm sure some wooden boards would float on a sea of mud.

"Great symbolism," Clyde agreed.

Absolutely.

"How do we get a crowd?" I asked.

"Well, there's got to be a press release."

"I'll write it," Karen said with a notable lack of enthusiasm.

"We can just tell Sal and Susie there'll be beer and food." Clyde added.

Sal and Susie were better resources for spreading out the word in our little town than radio or television. "We have to tell Lilly too."

"Right. A press release and some good word of food. Everyone will be there. We need to dress Bruno up." I knew that a candidate had to look good to be good.

"How?" Karen asked.

"I don't know. We'll figure it out. There'll have to be a stump speech."

"I can write that," Clyde said.

"Who'll deliver it? "

"You've got to do it, Jimmy," he added.

Well, I was the best choice.

"We'll have to say Bruno has laryngitis or something," Clyde suggested.

"Let's make it funny."

"Good."

"You know, Paolo might want to help." It was a thought that just kind of appeared in my mind. Karen was being very quiet. I should have paid attention.

"Do you think a chef can make dog biscuits. That doesn't seem right."

Gosh, Clyde seemed a little skeptical.

"How about cookies in the shape of dog biscuits?" I suggested.

"Cookies will be good, if he'll do it."

"Paolo's a great guy. And he has a sense of humor. He also might love the publicity."

"And it will help Bruno too," Clyde added.

"I'll ask him," I said. "And we can buy real dog biscuits for our canine friends." This was getting better as we went along. Carsone was going to be beside himself, which would take up a lot of room.

"Don't dog biscuits create a problem?" Clyde paused and frowned. I waited, moving a little to the front of my chair and leaning forward. "Most of the people in this town are likely to eat the dog biscuits too, particularly if they're not sober."

Most of them were rarely sober.

"Not our issue," I said. "We mark them. They eat them, most of our constituents who can read will get it right. The others proba-bly won't know the difference."

"I'm okay with that," Clyde said. He knew a problem solver when he saw one.

"What do we do now. How can we make this an even bigger joke?" I was enjoying this a lot. Looking at Karen's face, she wasn't.

"We do it seriously. Just like it is for real. We get campaign buttons and lawn signs. We use the slogan you made up?" Clyde said.

Huh?

"This town is going to the dogs."

"Right. Good. And I think we should ask Polly to introduce Bruno," I said. "It would be funny."

"Do you think he will do that?" Karen asked. I was glad she was getting involved, no matter how reluctantly.

I figured that Polly needed the exposure now that someone was running against him. We'd be killing two birds with one stone. I wasn't exactly clear that I might be one of the birds.

"Good idea. Maybe he will want to pass out some campaign gifts?" I was getting into this campaigning stuff.

"Do you think?"

"Polly and campaign gifts?" I said, with a lift in my voice.

"Sure. What if he gave out little vibrators inscribed 'Polly for City Council,'" Clyde suggested. He was smiling and laughing at the same time. This was really starting to tickle his fancy. His face was alight and the corners of his lips turned up.

"Well, he'd be front and center with his voting base," I observed. That was a terrible pun. Karen didn't laugh.

"Yeah, but it might lead to a really good climax." Clyde was all in.

That brought eye rolls from Karen, accompanied by a vigorous shake of the head.

"We need to have someone video tape the event. If we are going to do this, we should do it," Karen said. I think she finally had given up.

"Got it," Clyde said. "One of the law students can do it. I'll rent a camera."

"If Bruno wins, he can get the city to pay us back," I added.

Only kidding.

Chapter 11

"Sure I help you. Et is funny, what you are doing." Paolo had a big smile on his face. He was showing a lot of teeth.

"That's swell, Paolo. You know, you don't have to do this. It is a big ask."

"What es this 'big ask' you say?"

Paolo and I were sitting out of the rain, on the balcony of his hotel room on the Pointe. It was the best hotel in San Buenasara.

That's not hard since the competition is two down-scale chain motels on Highway 101 and 6 Airbnbs. Actually, it wasn't a bad hotel. The rooms were large and clean. They replaced the carpeting every three years or so and there were no rust stains in the tub.

And it had a great view out over the marina to the ocean. The storms had increased the waves and they were being tossed high over the breakwater. The effect was loud and dramatic.

"It means I'm asking you to do something that takes a lot of effort and isn't something you're obligated to do," I said. "Heck, you just came to town. You don't have a horse in this race."

"Jemmy, I do not understand. I have no horse. I could not bring horse from Etaly."

This was getting more complicated than I could handle. I decided to quit trying to apologize. I needed to bite my tongue. Always a difficult decision for a lawyer.

"No, Paolo, it is just a saying. What we call a colloquialism. It means there isn't a reason for you to do this. There is nothing for you to gain."

I don't want to be boring, but it was raining again. By the grace of God, it was a light, sheer rain and the wind wasn't blowing. It actually was rather pleasant. Paolo was sipping a glass of Barolo. I don't drink anymore, but I loved the deep red color. I noticed the vintage on the label. That certainly had not come from the hotel. I was drinking a glass of cranberry juice. Excellent cranberry juice, I might add. Perfectly aged.

Poalo took a sip of wine.

"I don'ta like these men who want to do bad things. We hav' many in my country. Always taking. Bad men."

"We call them politicians here," I said. "Let me define politician for you, Paolo. 'Poli,' Latin meaning 'many.' 'Tics,' meaning 'blood sucking vermin.'"

Paolo chuckled and held a finger up to the side of his mouth.

"I remember that, Jemmy. Es good. We have many such men in Etaly."

"Paolo, we appreciate your helping. It's a big joke. We'll get nothing out of it other than embarrassing Carsone and maybe getting someone else to run. We can't pay you."

"No, es also good for me too. Maka people like me here. Regular people. Always good. Care about our town. Keep et nice."

"Yeah, we care too."

"So, maybe I make some cookies. Shapa like dog biscuits. Maybe say 'Vote for Bruno.' I do Italian Wedding Cookies. Great treat."

"Wonderful, Paolo. I thought you were just a great chef. I didn't know you baked."

"I lova to bake. But I learn being chef from great teachers."

"You went to cooking school?"

"Greata teachers in kitchen. We learn by doing cooking. Hard work. Work many hours. Hot. Very strict, but good? Took many years before I open my own restaurant."

"Are these cookies you're going to do hard to make?"

"Jemmy, all good food es hard to make. But, I do it, okay? You think people lika anise?

"I don't know what anise is, Paolo."

"Tasta like black licorice."

"Gosh, I don't know. I don't like the taste myself."

The wind shifted and a feather of rain touched my cheek. I stuck out my tongue to catch it. Paolo laughed.

"I do that when I am little boy also. You little boy at heart, Jemmy. Es good."

That nailed me pretty well. I hadn't pulled a prank like this since I was 12.

"Okay, I make soma with almond. Also very good."

"When did you learn to bake?"

"I bake before I can reach table. Before I become great chef. Mamma, she great baker. She teach me. Paolo become great baker too. You love cookies. I make special for Bruno. How many cookie you need?"

"Gosh, we don't know. A hundred?" That was optimistic, I thought.

Paolo lifted his hands into the air. "Okay, I make hundred cookie."

The rain started to pick up and it was growing cold. Paolo shivered.

"Maybe we go inside now, Jemmy."

Paolo and I adjourned to his sitting room. I carefully closed the sliding door behind us. He took a seat on the couch overlooking the marina. I took the chair to his left. We put our glasses down on the coffee table.

"That's great, Paolo. The campaign party is day after tomorrow."

"No problem. I use your kitchen?"

"Sure, but it isn't a very good stove."

I may have been overstating that. Karen has many wonderful qualities. Cooking isn't one of them. Nor one of mine. We never used the stove. I hope it worked. We supported the local economy. We ate out a lot.

"Our stove, at home, when I grow up. It burn wood. I cook on anything. I am great chef."

"How much money do you need for ingredients and supplies, Paolo?"

"Es nothing" Paolo spread his arms wide. "I pay. I love idea of Bruno. He good dog?"

"Bruno's the best."

"Maybe he get elected. Can become important customer. Celebrity." Paolo laughed a hearty laugh. I couldn't help liking this cheerful little man. Even if he went on kissing me.

"Paolo, you have a wonderful sense of humor. Bruno would be a great mayor. But I think you're barking up the wrong tree here." I couldn't resist. I'm hanging my head.

"You care, maybe I tell my publicity people I bake for Bruno. People may find it, how you say, amusing. Go on internet, all over. Famoose chef go all out for underdog."

"Sure. Any publicity you can get will only help."

"Okay, hundred cookies, day after tomorrow."

"Will you come to the party?"

"I come. You introduce me to friends. I want to make friends here. My restaurant is always place for friends and families in Etaly."

"How about letting us introduce you from the stage?"

I had no idea if there would be a stage. There had to be one. I'd just said it. There'd have to be something. I better talk to Clyde. There probably should be a microphone. Darn, it. This was really complicated.

Chapter 12

I HURRIED BACK TO the office. There was a lot to do. This campaign business was difficult. But, I'm a master. I knew the way.

The way was to delegate. To Clyde.

At least I wasn't wet. Not on the inside at least. I had on a raincoat and had taken an umbrella. I'm a quick learner.

As I came in, I took off the raincoat in the reception room and hung it in the closet. I hung the umbrella over the closet bar by its handle. They dripped on the carpet, but no one could see it. I figured the puddle would dry eventually.

Pamela was on a break or lost. I went directly into Clyde's office. I was a little breathless after all the exercise. It is several blocks from the Pointe and I had walked fast.

"Clyde, Paolo's going to help," I said in an enthusiastic tone.

Clyde looked up from his computer and swiveled in his chair towards me.

"Glad to hear it. He seems like a nice guy."

"A really good man, I think. He's making cookies. Italian Wedding Cookies that will be shaped like dog biscuits. Whatever Italian Wedding Cookies are."

"With anise?"

Show off.

"I think we should order dog biscuits, like we talked about," I continued gesturing with an open hand. "We can stick them in little packages. Tie them with a 'Bruno for Mayor' ribbon. Can we get 'Bruno for Mayor' ribbons printed before tomorrow?"

Clyde picked up his pen and made a note on the legal pad sitting on the corner of his desk.

"I don't know, Boss, but I'll find out. You gotta know, I'm not tying a couple hundred packages of cookies and dog biscuits." He put down his pen. "I've got standards too."

"No, I don't expect you to tie up dog biscuits." The old lawyer's trick of the non-inclusive. I could ask him to tie packages of cookies without breaking my word. I had only mentioned dog biscuits. Never make promises you won't keep. But then a thought occurred to me.

Hey, that's not as unusual as you seem to think.

"Maybe we can get some kids from Karen's law school class to help. Working on a campaign will look good on their resumes. They won't have to say Bruno is a dog. They can tie the bags."

Clyde looked askance. Maybe he didn't think being a campaign worker for a dog would send the right message on a resume.

"Come on Clyde, it's not a lie. They don't have to mention Bruno. It's a sin of omission, at worst. I would never tell a lie. I'm a lawyer."

Clyde's eyes went wide and shook his head. He was trying to restrain a laugh. Not very successfully. Maybe he was just choking.

"Clyde, please quit laughing. It's unseemly. The kids can even pass out buttons too. Can we get buttons?"

"Already ordered buttons. Posters too. Got six cases of beer and little hot dogs wrapped in dough." That's what made Clyde a good lawyer. He was two steps ahead all the time. I know, I'm a great lawyer, but I was saving my energy for the campaign.

Thank God for Clyde.

"Don't we need some other stuff? A stage?"

"I ordered a platform. A microphone too."

I was getting the sneaking suspicion my partner was smarter than I was. Obviously, that couldn't be. He must have done this before somewhere. I couldn't be expected to think of everything. I was obviously distracted by the importance of speaking with Paolo.

Look, I realize I'm complicated. A weird mix of bravado and insecurity.

I grew up poor. Not skid row poor. Just ordinary poor. Mom raised me and my brother by working 12 hours a day in a little grocery store. My father died in a car crash when I was eight. He was a drunk.

My brother got the brains. He's a college professor in Midland, Texas. He teaches economics. I didn't envy him his position, even though he got to learn a foreign language. I personally never wanted to speak Texan.

I got the good looks and charm. We were never close.

I wasn't a great student, but you know how California is. I went to a community college where I was better with the girls than with my books. That was okay by me. I got laid a lot. I made it into Cal State Long Beach by the skin of my teeth which is the same way I got out. A political science major. Politics appealed to me. As far as I could tell, you were paid for doing nothing. I felt I could be good at the job.

Oh, and I got married in my last year in college. She was a looker. Carrie Moss. It didn't last. Four years, over and out. I wasn't communicative enough. Ms. Moss hated my sense of humor. And I left the toilet seat up.

I think she may have become perturbed when she got up in the middle of the night to use the bathroom. It was quiet for a moment or two. Then I heard a splash.

I didn't even know she knew some of those words. It may have been unhelpful that I was giggling uncontrollably when she returned to our soon to be ex-conjugal bed.

After graduating I found myself well qualified to do a variety of janitorial tasks. Actually, I worked on a lot of construction jobs. I hated it. It was really hard, physical work. And I got my hands dirty.

That was my motivation for going to night school to study law. Western States. I think it's accredited now. Law was as close to politics as I could get.

After passing the bar, I finally landed a job with the public defender's office. It took about three months. It's a great way to diet.

I'm proud of the fact I passed the bar on the very first time that I really applied myself. The third time I took it if I recall correctly. Those five years with the public defender led me to being the great lawyer I am today.

But it all left some scars.

"Did Polly agree to introduce Bruno?" I asked.

"Karen spoke to Polly. He loves the idea."

"I'm glad he's so enthusiastic. How long did it take him to stop laughing?

Clyde held up five fingers, and chuckled.

"Did you talk to him about his own campaign stuff."

"I sure did, Boss. We is here to please." Clyde's face broke out in a smile that bordered on a laugh. His smile showed perfect teeth. He thinks his dialect is funny. Actually, so do I. Sometimes.

"Polly already thought of that," Clyde continued with a lilt in his voice. "Mini-vibrators. Had them in stock. Getting them printed as we speak. I suggested he have them printed upside down so people would read them while they were in use."

I thought about that and immediately banished it from my thoughts. I sat up straight.

"Did he think that six cases of beer would be enough?" I asked. This was important. Our friends and constituents would not respond well to being denied their fair share of alcohol. Their idea of a fair share was somewhat larger than others might consider normal.

"He thinks that most of the people will be so high they won't be able to find the beer." A flash of lightning put an exclamation point on his point.

"Let's order pretzels and nuts. Okay?" What would they do without my insights?

"On it, Boss." Clyde picked up his pen and made another note.

"Clyde, you're doing a great job." Always compliment your workers. It encourages them. "And, don't call me 'Boss.'"

Whew, after all my hard work, I needed a nap. Being a master organizer is hard.

Chapter 13

"Hı."

The microphone squawked like someone was strangling a parrot. A guy rushed up to the edge of the stage and turned a few dials. He nodded to me. I tried again.

"You all know Polly Polivnakov," I said, turning and gesturing with an open hand at Polly who was sitting at the rear of the platform with Clyde and Karen. Karen had Bruno on her lap.

Ninety-five people burst into applause and cheers. They stamped on the wooden boards under their feet. It was cool and cloudy. We got lucky with the weather, but according to our weatherman, it was unsettled. And there were some nasty looking clouds poking their noses our way. It was still light out, but the light was subdued.

Polly stood up and was waving both hands, turning this way and that. Judging by the loopy smile on his face he was enjoying himself.

There was a cold breeze that carried the distinct odor of pot. Not to put too fine a point on it, a few more minutes exposure and we would all be in the same boat. Given the weather, having a boat wouldn't be a bad idea.

The cheers and stomping went on. Our friends were feeling frisky. Probably because they were high. Or drunk. Or, most likely, both. Some of them were dancing around with their hands over their head. The platform was vibrating with the movement of the wooden floorboards. There were so many people, our end of the wooden expanse was rising, so everything seemed a little downhill.

I had no doubt they could hear us all over town. I bet they could even hear us in the Carsone for Mayor office.

I was behind a little podium set on a raised platform and I was holding a microphone close to my mouth. Clyde had done an incredible job. We were at the Dog Park, standing on what looked like a very large dance floor with the raised platform standing at the far end. I prayed the floor wouldn't float away. A wooden path ran from the square floor out to the concrete carpark. It was getting cold and people were zipping up their jackets.

I spotted several friends in the crowd. I waved to one or two. I recognized many more faces. But there were a lot of people here I didn't know. I guess they were here for the beer. After all, this was a rally to nominate a dog to run for mayor. Or maybe they just needed a good laugh.

I held up my hands for silence. I wanted to get this over with before it started raining again and put a damper on things.

"Yes, yes. Polly, the man who stands, or perhaps lays, at the center of our hearts in our little town. The one who has tried over the years to bring comfort to those who are alone and to make upstanding those of you who couple. And he has the best shop windows ever. Pussy Galore is a landmark to all of us. A polestar in the darkness of our coming election."

A gust of wind made me pull the lapels of my jacket a little tighter towards my throat. I was dressed to the nines in pressed jeans and a blue blazer. Karen had selected my blue pocket handkerchief. My boots would have blinded me if I looked down. Sal had trimmed me up earlier in the afternoon and I was shining like a star.

"Polly is running for reelection to our City Council and we have asked him to speak tonight. He has served you well for eight years and will serve you well into the future. You could say his career has been dedicated to servicing you."

I was getting a kick out of all the double entendres. I suspected our friends would be too if they understood them. I looked back at Polly who had taken his seat again. Polly had on an open shirt over faded blue jeans, with a green wool jacket that had leather buttons. He was a beanpole of a guy and looked more like a college professor than a pornographer.

"Before I ask Polly to come up here, I want you to know Polly has provided a little gift for each of you. Please take one as you leave. Or even two if you need it.

I paused. "Shame on you," I said, widening my eyes. There was a smattering of titillating laughter.

"They have batteries and are ready for immediate use. Polly wants each of you to have a vibrant future with a great City Council."

I paused again dramatically for maybe 20 seconds. It seemed much longer. As I paused, I moved my head from left to right, looking over the audience. The silence grew. Then I turned and made a sweeping gesture with my arm. The one not holding the microphone, if you were wondering.

"Now ladies and gentlemen (and whomever else might be out there)," I whispered away from the microphone, "please welcome Polly Polivnakov."

Applause and whoops burst out as Polly rose and walked slowly to the podium. I could tell from the look on his face he was anxious. In all his preceding elections, I don't think he ever had to give a speech in public. I stepped to the side and handed him the microphone. He looked at it as if it might bite him. We had been going over this with him. It had taken an hour and a half for him to hold the mic steady.

He took the microphone, hesitantly raised it towards his lips and spoke in a whisper. I retreated to my seat in the back.

"Louder," someone shouted. "We can't hear you."

To Polly's credit, he didn't run, although I swear I saw the thought flash across his face. He raised the microphone closer to his lips and spoke louder. Sweat broke out on his forehead.

"Hi everybody. I'm a little nervous." He definitely sounded it. He stuttered a little.

"I know a lot of you, but seeing you all here at once scares me. I'm just a small shopkeeper, but I do care about our town and who we are. I just want to help."

There were encouraging yells from some of the people in the crowd. "We love you, Polly."

As he got going, he seemed to be getting more confidant. His voice seemed stronger and more even.

"I've never had to campaign before. Believe me, no one wants this job. I mean, you have to deal with all of you. And you all know how that is."

There was a lot of laughs. People really did love Polly.

"But now someone wants my seat. I don't even really know him. Who is he? When did he move here? What does he want?"

We had done several hours of research and worked with Polly on his talking points. The only concern was that Polly had to talk. But he was doing great.

"I had to look him up on the internet. I can do that now. My two-year-old niece showed me how." People chuckled. A couple of them expressed raucous doubts. "This man moved here two or three years ago. He sells annuities. I mean there's nothing wrong with selling annuities, but how does that prepare you for doing what you—what we—want? That is what I think I do. At least what I've tried to do on the City Council."

"Yes. Yes." The voices came from several places in the crowd.

"He's spending a lot of money on his campaign. I have no idea where it's coming from," Polly said, following his talking points. He was doing great.

"Maybe he makes a lot of money. But not that I can see. "

Polly lowered the mike and took a deep breath and glanced back. I gave him an encouraging fist gesture and nod. Polly lifted the mike and started again.

"I don't get people spending a lot of money unless they want something. I can tell you, it's not the salary or the perks from being on City Council. It's pretty much a pain in the ass. Do you know how long some of you can talk?"

Polly paused again. His timing was good.

"I guess whoever it is who is providing the money just wants our town. But what about you and me?"

I started clapping. A lot of people joined in.

"That's all I have to say. I would like it if you would vote for me. I want to stay on the City Council and continue to be your quality adult store in our town. My door is always open, and, as you know, there are places inside to hide. Gosh, I didn't know I could talk this much."

Polly really looked abashed. He'd made a whole speech. It made sense. People seemed to like it. They seemed to like him. He stopped and looked around at Karen and me. I gave him my best smile and a confirming nod.

Then he continued. I was touched that he remembered why he was up there.

"But I'm really up here to introduce our candidate for mayor."

This was the speech Clyde and I wrote. We printed it out in large bold letters so Polly could read it.

"I know our candidate well. I like him. You like him. He's down to earth. Right down to earth." Polly stepped from behind the podium, bent his knees and lowered his flat hand two feet from the ground.

"I could say 'look at his opponent,' but darn it, why would I want you to look at something that ugly. Some people say that Bruno's opponent is two faced. Bruno wants to assure you that, no matter what his other faults, Walter Carsone is not two-faced. If he were two-faced, he would never choose to wear the one he's wearing.

That drew a laugh.

"Bruno's candidacy stands on its own. He has his feet planted solidly on the ground. All four of them. He cares."

Lots of clapping and laughter. Our little joke was bringing a lot of fun to our small town. Carsone would be furious. Polly finished with a bang.

"Now don't go and bark up the wrong tree." He paused and turned, the microphone still at his lips. "Here is our candidate, Bruno Harris."

I stood up and Karen handed me Bruno. With him under my

arm, I walked to the front of the platform and took the microphone from Polly. Bruno surveyed the crowd. He was a veteran. After all, he had donated the Bruno Harris Dog Park upon which we stood and participated in its dedication.

I thanked Polly and glanced up at the sky. The clouds were now covering the pale moon. I hurried on.

"I'm Jimmy Harris, Bruno's campaign manager. You all know me. I've bailed most of you out of jail." That provoked a few straggled chuckles.

"Bruno is having a problem with speaking tonight; vocal cords, you know. He has asked me to speak for him. "

I looked down at Bruno and opened my eyes wide.

"But you do approve of everything I am about to say, boy, don't you?"

"Woof." Right on que.

"There you have it. Bruno approves of every word," I said it with conviction.

"We need to protect our way of life. Do we want to be Rodeo Drive by the sea? To have cars, day and night? To have a town filled with strangers? I mean they're strange.

"Now there is nothing wrong with strangers. But isn't it better to know everyone. To be comfortable with where you live. You can go meet strangers anyplace. They're all over. You can even meet strangers here, if you try. Many of us may be strange, but we are not strangers."

I lowered the microphone and paused to let that sink in.

"Our opponent has suggested that he will lower taxes, improve services and increase law enforcement. That is pretty appealing. Particularly the lower taxes bit. Maybe not the policing so much. But how much and at what cost? Where is he going to get the money? I ask you, look into your soul. If they close Pussy Galore…and they will, you can bet on that…what will become of Polly. What will become of you?"

I was interrupted by the grumbling sounds from the crowd. I think they were getting it.

"Bruno only asks that you think about that. If you want our way of life to go on, please…"

Here I stopped for dramatic impact. I'm a ham at heart.

"This may be dumb, but I've got to say it. 'Unleash the future.'"

Someone started shouting, "Bruno, Bruno!" People joined in. Everyone was shouting and laughing. People really do like Bruno.

I shouted into the microphone above the roar. And raised my hand for silence.

Before I could speak, a well-endowed young woman in a halter top and tight jeans rushed towards the platform. She threw a pair of panties towards me, screaming, "I love you, Bruno." The panties hit me in the face and fell to the floor, provoking laughter. I was laughing too. Bruno just looked interested. I held up my hands to quiet our friends.

"Now there is a voter who is prepared to give", I said. "But we want to give to you tonight. We have a gift for you. On your way out, next to the miniature vibrators so generously provided by your candidate for City Council, Polly Polivnakov, help yourself to a delicious Bruno cookie baked by the gourmet chef, our friend from Italy, Paolo Marino. "

I pointed to Paolo in the crowd. He waved back, giving me a big smile. Then he put his hands together over his head like a victorious wrestler and turning, shook them, much to the delight of everyone.

"Paolo is famous in Italy. He has two Michelin stars. He wants to open a restaurant here in our little town. Paolo wants San Buenasara to remain the treasure that it is. We hope you do too."

People around Paolo were shouting and slapping him on the back. He hugged some of them. Some of them I would have liked to hug too.

I raised the microphone to my mouth again and spoke into it.

"These cookies are usually called Italian Wedding Cookies, but for tonight, they are called Bruno Cookies." I paused, then continued.

"The vibrators are the little oblong things. The cookies are shaped like a dog biscuit so you can tell them apart. And there are real dog biscuits. Don't get any of them confused."

Into the ensuing laughter, I shouted into the microphone, "This town is going to the dogs! Vote for Bruno!"

And the crowd shouted back. That's when the first wet blob of rain hit me on the face.

Chapter 14

OUR ANNOUNCEMENT OF BRUNO'S candidacy caused a stir. We sent the tape of the festivities along with a news release to the local TV station, our weekly newspaper and the *Los Angeles Times*. I admit, the latter was a stretch, but hey.

The TV station ran excerpts from the tape. It must have been a slow news day. Or maybe Laura Evenwell, the anchor for the evening news, liked Bruno. Bruno is a popular fellow.

Laura Evenwell was a petite blond lady who was handsome without being pretty. She was in her early thirties. Since we were probably the 150th largest television market of the 212 markets in the United States, we were lucky to have her, although I did wonder what her future held. She brought gravitas and poise to the news. Her experience showed. She was good at her job.

The newscast cut away from my announcement of Bruno's candidacy to a shot of the campaign headquarters of Walter Carsone. The place was bustling. Laura was holding a microphone in front of an upset, balding, corpulent man.

At least you might conclude he was upset since he seemed to be foaming at the mouth. His face was red and his lips were curled down. He seemed to be gnashing his teeth. Walter Carsone in the flesh, in his case a lot of it, was standing with a certain tension in his body. He was trying to smile at Laura. Laura, like any investigative reporter, knows when she's on to a good thing.

There was a lot of noise and bustle in the background. Laura leaned in closer to Carsone.

"Chief Carsone," she said, raising her voice, "how do you view the entry into the mayor's race of what I can only describe as an unusual opponent? Perhaps an unprecedented opponent. I do not remember a dog ever running for public office."

"This is a sick joke being made by a disreputable and disbarred lawyer." He was a bit on the loud side. Laura seemed to step back a bit so as not to be caught in the burst of spittle spraying from his mouth.

Besides, that wasn't fair. I wasn't disbarred. Yes, I was reproved by the Bar, but I can explain that. It wasn't my fault. Well, maybe a little. I've mentioned McNulty.

McNulty used to be my partner in Los Angeles. Things weren't going so hot and McNulty wasn't an honest lawyer. When a client pays you $2,000 in cash and you count it and discover an extra hundred, an honest lawyer splits it with his partner.

One night McNulty came home from a late meeting with lipstick on his fly. Now McNulty's a real charmer. He could talk the birds out of the trees. His explanation was sheer melody. It sang. And Mrs. McNulty, Darlene, is an understanding woman.

She didn't divorce him. That's the bad news. Instead, she made every day a living hell for him. And spent him into the ground. I could almost feel sorry for the guy. "Almost" is the operative word in that sentence.

McNulty was stealing from the client's trust account, which is a big no-no in the legal business. I didn't notice. It didn't help that I was drinking at the time. I mean, hey, I was under a lot of stress.

The firm had cash problems. And one of my erstwhile clients, a not very nice drug dealer, felt that I had not done well by him. Darn, I got him a cell with a nice southern exposure and everything. Ingrate. He was threatening me. Far worse, he was threatening Karen. They were ugly threats. I was worried sick.

The bar didn't take well to McNulty raiding the cookie jar. McNulty got disbarred. It took some doing to convince the

Disciplinary Board that I had nothing to do with the theft and I really had no idea what was happening. Finally, they recognized I was a totally oblivious idiot.

I get a public reproval and free membership in the State Bar's substance abuse program.

Alas, Walter Carsone doesn't like me. Perhaps it is because, I've, on more than one occasion, called him a twit. Some people just can't handle constructive criticism.

Chief Carsone epitomized what a police chief should be. That is, if bald, fat and lazy is now the standard.

He ascended to his role as chief of police the hard way. Through nepotism. He immediately proved his worth by ruthlessly crushing an epidemic of jay walking that was running rampant in San Buenasara.

Our paths have crossed several times, many more than I would have liked. He was involved in the investigation of the Janet Mason murder. Not in a meaningful way, but he was there. And that's the naked truth. I know because I was naked at the time.

He completely ignored it when a crazed husband shot at me. And his appearance in the case involving Wee Willy's death made the FBI laugh.

Laura Evenwell nodded sagely at Carsone. "Do you take this as a commentary on your campaign?" To her credit, she asked the question with a straight face.

"I do not!" Carsone said, bridling at the question. "As I said," he visibly drew himself up and sharpened his voice, "it is just a sick joke that undermines the sanctity of the election process and therefore the very root of our democracy. That ... lawyer," he said making the word "lawyer" sleezy, which isn't all that hard, "should be tried for treason."

"Chief Carsone, don't you think that is a little extreme?"

"No. What these people are doing is vile. They are attempting to mock me, but I stand for the defense of our American rights. I know that my supporters, fine, honest, loyal people, see me as a true patriot."

The segment cut back to a shot of me holding Bruno.

"Mr. Harris, Chief Carsone has made some very serious allegations against you." Laura Evenwell also had come to our office to interview me.

"Yes, he has. All of which are untrue." Except maybe the joke part. "But I believe the voters should get to decide who can best serve them." I looked down at Bruno.

"Bruno, do you have any thoughts?

Laura turned and extended the microphone towards Bruno.

"Woof," he said. Then Bruno licked her hand. She giggled.

I looked at Bruno, admiring both his sagacity and his succinctness. And kissing up to the press. All admirable qualities in a politician.

Chapter 15

"BOSS, DID YOU SEE the newspaper this morning?" Clyde had a concerned look on his face.

I was up bright and early, as usual. Bright was when the sun was well established in the sky. That is, if it wasn't raining, which it was. Early was 10:00 and I was right on time.

I had just walked into the office. The commute down the stairs was pretty quick. That was the good news. The bad news was that I couldn't claim to be caught in traffic, so that excuse was out the window, in the rain.

"No. Anything interesting? When it rains, I love the pitter patter on the roof. But it had been more thump, thump, the past few weeks. There was the occasional bolt of lightning to show us God was having a good time.

"They have a front-page editorial on the rally yesterday. The publisher wrote it." Clyde held the paper up in front of his face.

I felt perky in spite of the rain. The rally where we announced Bruno's entry into the race for mayor had been a very upbeat event. The cookies especially. We got a lot of laughs. And Bruno seemed happy.

"The *Los Angeles Times* has a front-page editorial on us?" Wow, this was better than I thought.

I could barely see the marina over his shoulder. The windows were awash. The boats looked cold and desolate, the rain dancing on their decks. I was glad I wasn't on board one of them. They were rocking in the swells. I almost felt sea sick just looking at them. I sat down across from Clyde.

"Not the *Times*," Clyde said. "You've got some kind of delusions, Boss. It was the *Journal*." Clyde would know about my delusions, of grandeur and otherwise.

The *San Buenasara Journal* was our weekly paper. This was a special edition.

"Well, that's still okay. I mean these are the people who we want to reach, right?"

"I'm not so sure. You better read it." Clyde held the paper out to me. Hesitated, then pulled it back.

"They say any publicity is good, if they spell your name right," I said it with noticeable restraint. I wanted to encourage him to come across with the newspaper.

"Actually, no." He emphasized 'no.'

"They didn't spell my name right."

"They did. That's the problem?"

"I don't get it?" I said, looking up from the paper in Clyde's hand to his face.

"That's why you should read it. Actually, let me read you a small excerpt." Clyde drew the paper back towards him and his eyes flicked down the page. Then he nodded and started to read.

This rally was repugnant to our democracy and a blackeye for the town of San Buenasara. To run a dog against an outstanding candidate like Walter Carsone is in utter bad taste, even as a joke. And it must be a joke.

The joker is a local lawyer named James Emerson Harris, a man of dubious reputation. Mr. Harris was accused of the murder of William Witkowski, the founder of Wee Willy's after Mr. Witkowski made him president of the company.

Mr. Harris, a man of ruthless ambition but little skill, was released on a legal technicality without ever standing trial.

Hey, sure they arrested me for Willy's murder. That was a mistake. I told them so, but nobody listens to me. I was in jail for months until they discovered how dumb it was. They didn't even apologize.

It wasn't a good time for me. You wouldn't like the food in jail either. But it came out okay. I mean the city even settled the case Clyde brought against them. That's why the Law Offices of James Emerson Harris represents the City of San Buenasara pursuant to a twenty-year guaranteed contract.

And, yes, I had been the president of Wee Willy's. That was the local company that grew and distributed marijuana. I don't know if it was those other lawyers or the FBI that was to blame for ruining the company and hurting our little town, but it wasn't me. I had inherited a real mess, and I did a great job in keeping Wee Willy's afloat. Sure, we might have had to close it down. You know, in a good way. But the FBI insisted upon keeping it open, actually put up the money. They wanted to run a sting. Then they dropped me and Wee Willy's like the stub of a marijuana joint when they were through with us.

Clyde went on with his reading in that damn sonorous voice of his.

And of course, Mr. Harris is infamous for his involvement in the murder of the beloved television star, Janet Mason.

Now wait a minute. That is totally unfair. I risked my life trying to help Janet Mason. I mean, not on purpose, but I did risk my life.

Mr. Harris's involvement in these events make him singularly unqualified to run for public office. And what could be behind nominating a dog but his desire for power. Obviously, he could not run under his own name given his dreadful background and reputation.

If nominated, I will not run. And if elected, I will not serve. I just made that up.

Clyde just couldn't stop.

To hide behind a dog is disgraceful. But we believe, not beneath him.

Let me just say Bruno isn't big enough to hide behind or tall enough to hide beneath. Leave it at that.

"Wow, those guys can't take a joke. Why do you think the publisher wrote that editorial?"

"I believe he's been bought and paid for by Mr. Carsone or the folks who are financing him. His bread is buttered on that side. He is going to make heaps of money on the development of San Buenasara. A lot of new advertising. And it doesn't appear that Mr. Carsone has a good sense of humor."

"And that's an excerpt? You mean it goes on?" I ran my hand through what hair I had left.

"You have to settle in for a good read, Boss. I only read you the complimentary parts."

My face would have slid off if it weren't so tightly attached

"This isn't very good for the law firm, is it."

"It's not so good for you, either."

"Do you think Bruno should withdraw?"

"You know, Jimmy, I've given that some thought." Clyde leaned back in his chair and looked up at the ceiling for a moment. Then he lowered his head and looked at me. "I think we shouldn't withdraw right now. It would seem like an admission. Like there was something you wanted to hide."

Well, I did actually. I had quite a bit to hide. Not about the election or anything like that. I've just led an adventurous life. I don't want anyone to become jealous.

"I agree," I said. "Let's wait a bit. When things calm down, we can let it just slip away. Bruno can announce he wants to spend more time with his family.

Chapter 16

THINGS STARTED MOVING A little faster than I had anticipated. It was later that day when Paolo Marino knocked on the door to the conference room.

"Come in," I called out. Paolo poked his head in.

"Paolo, come in. I wanted to thank you."

I made a 'come in' gesture with my hand. As he walked in, I opened my mouth to continue, but before I could say anything, Paolo broke in. He was excited.

"Jemmy, I just get call from Gilbert Sachs," Paolo said. Sure, he was excited, but, he was Italian. His eyes were dancing.

"Investment guy? Goldman Sachs?" I wanted to show Paolo I was a sophisticated man of superior insight. He didn't seem impressed. He shook his head and used his hand to try to push away my comment.

"No, no, Jemmy, Gilbert Sachs. More important. He is food critic for *New York Times*. Everyone knows."

Maybe not everyone.

"He know of me. Say he heard I am opening restaurant in San Buenasara. Want to come meet. I told him I would cook."

"Paolo, that's great."

"Jemmy, I have no place to cook."

I immediately deduced that this was a problem.

"Ah." I am a man of few words.

"You let me cook here."

"Paolo, you baked the cookies here. You know we only have a small kitchen. It's almost non-existent." And almost brand new. I was fortunate Karen had never desired to cook for me after she served me her first attempt. I think she probably poisoned her prior three boyfriends, which is why I got lucky.

"You know, I cook anywhere. We serve in conference room."

"But we're running Bruno's campaign out of there, Paolo. There's stuff all over the walls. The whole office looks like a campaign headquarters."

We had taken down our picture and covered the walls with campaign posters and slogans. There were posters of Bruno shaking hands and posters of him with campaign slogans written underneath. The one I liked best was the picture of Karen holding Bruno, but I'm prejudiced.

Paolo had done a great job for us. I was concerned. I didn't want him to mess up with this big-time food critic.

"Is okay. Believe me, he taste my food, he be in heaven. Maybe heaven with posters. It be good. Maybe he even mention Bruno in review. He will help campaign."

That would have been an interesting thought except that we intended to drop out. I didn't want to step on Paolo's enthusiasm. And it couldn't hurt, could it. He probably wouldn't even mention Bruno.

"Sure," I said. Anything for old Paolo.

"We serve my Bruno cookies with coffee. Give him whole box." Paolo had made beautiful Italian wedding cookies that looked just like dog biscuits for us to use to announce his entry into the mayoral race and for his campaign. We took home a few. Get your share first is my motto. They had been a great success. And I ate all the ones we took home. After all, I'm the campaign manager. I need to keep up my strength.

"He want to come tomorrow night. You and Karen come. Gilbert, he like Karen. He be impressed with her. She become lawyer."

"Clyde, he come too. He most impressive. Gilbert see I am important man."

What am I, chopped liver? Is that even an Italian dish?

"What about Bruno?" Now I was being a wise-ass. A wise-ass with a big smile on his cheeks. Hey, he pushed me to it.

That caused him pause. He stopped talking and put his hand to his chin and lowered his head. I waited.

"You have great thought, Jemmy," he said looking up. "Make dinner most different. Put handkerchief on Bruno with colors of Italian flag. Bruno's picture be on the wall. Can Bruno shake Gilbert's hand?"

"Absolutely." Bruno had learned to lift his paw often in his unrelenting attempt to express his common nature. Bruno is an elitist at heart. Ask me. But, he always puts his best paw forward if he wants something. Usually food. Now he wanted votes too. I wasn't so sure about press coverage.

"What are you going to cook?" I wondered what he could prepare on such short notice. We did have a lot of fresh vegetables in San Buenasara. And there was a first-class meat market in San Luis. But there wasn't a lot of gourmet stuff.

"I maybe make him my famoose Bistecca all Fiorintina ana beautiful pasta, maybe Tagliatelle with Bolognese. I have it with the perfect lettle zucchini blossoms. I create wonderful dish. He will luv et."

I was pretty sure I would love it too. I was certain Bruno would. It was food.

Chapter 17

PAOLO WAS RIGHT ABOUT Gilbert Sachs being impressed with Karen. But he didn't even know how right he was.

Karen was in her first year of law school. I understood how important that was to her and how impressive it actually is.

I needn't point out again that Karen is beautiful. I thought so the first time I met her. She was incredible. We were introduced by a friend. No one had ever focused that much energy on me. The concentration in her eyes just gripped me.

We talked for four hours straight. They closed up the bar around us. All of our friends had left. We hadn't noticed.

That was 16 years ago. I was a mature 32. Karen was 23. I took her home that night. I didn't even try to hit on her. Okay, I did think about it.

We moved in together two months later. I knew why I was there. I had no idea why she was. With all my bluster, I do have some self-doubt. Uh, forget I said that.

I had even less of an idea 14 months later. We got married in a little park overlooking Lake Hollywood. Just a few friends and a guy to say the words.

The law practice was good. We had money. Karen never wanted children. Things were grand.

Karen had never finished college. She was clearly bright enough and she was an avid reader. It didn't make any sense. So, about a year after we got married, we were in our little apartment in Koreatown, standing in the kitchen. We weren't cooking. That was an act that never took place in our kitchen. Other acts took place, but not cooking.

We were unpacking little boxes of Chinese takeout. I looked over at her and asked her why she never graduated. She changed the subject.

That got me curious, so a month later, I asked again. She said something about not liking it and changed the subject again.

Hey, I'm a trained lawyer. That makes me a pain in the ass. So, a few months after that, I asked her again.

"I wasn't good enough," she said.

"Good enough at what?"

"Studying, I guess."

"You never wanted to go back?" I asked

She shook her head, but I was looking at her face. Her face wasn't saying the same thing.

"That wasn't exactly why you left school, was it?" I said.

She went quiet and just stood there. I could see the pain around her eyes.

"Jimmy, I've never talked about it. To anyone. I'm ashamed."

"Darling, first, I'm not anyone. There is nothing you could tell me that would matter. Except, maybe, if you were really a man. Then we'd have to discuss it."

She threw a dish towel at my head. But at least she smiled.

"Whatever it is, whatever happened, tell me. I promise you I am ashameder than you are."

"My father was a drunk."

"You never talked about him." I put my hand on her arm. A tear rolled down her cheek. I didn't mention that my own father had problems.

"I had gotten into Michigan State on a full scholarship and I was working at night as a waitress to pay for my room and board. My dad thought it was a waste of time. My mom thought I should be bringing in money for her and the family."

"Your parents didn't approve."

"I wanted to be a doctor. It was all I ever wanted. And I was good at the course work. I got the highest grade in Biology they had ever given. And I have great hands."

I can attest to that.

"Then, one day, my dad didn't come home. He just disappeared. I tried to ignore it, but my mom kept calling. 'She was starving.' 'She was going to be evicted.' 'She was sick.' She was good at sounding desperate. Better than at anything else."

"So, you quit school."

"Yeah, I did. I came home and went to work. My older brothers were both working. But they had Mom figured out. They stayed as far away from her as they could. They knew Mom wanted some-one to take care of her and that she would suck every ounce of juice out of their lives if they let her."

"Were they right?"

"Yes. I remember reading a phrase once about a place where 'hope goes to die'. That was my house. I stuck it out for 18 months. Mom was never well. I don't think she could be well. She always said she wanted to work, but somehow, she never did."

"And you were the only thing saving her and she was so grateful."

"No, that's the funny thing. She wasn't. She worshipped my brothers. If they sent a card, they were so thoughtful. I was her daughter. She expected it of me. I couldn't take it. So, I just left."

"What happened?"

She looked up into my face. "To me, or to my mother?"

"I never met your mother." I moved my hand and let it rest on her back. I could feel her shallow breathing.

"She died before we met."

"Did that make you feel guilty?"

"No." But Karen became still. "But I guess the funny thing is, I think I felt guilty about not feeling guilty."

"What did you do when you moved out?" I asked. I was trying really hard to be casual. I wanted to know and I thought it would be good for Karen too.

"I tried to go back to school. My scholarship had lapsed. When I reapplied, they told me I didn't qualify. I couldn't concentrate. I lasted two months. I gave up."

"But it's not too late to go back to school and finish your degree."

"Maybe. Or maybe I can do what Clyde did and become a lawyer."

And that is exactly what she did after we married last year. She would give Clyde a real run for his money. And I would continue to do what I always do. As little as possible. You should always play to your strengths.

Chapter 18

I WAS ON MY way back from the Lilly Pad where I had had a satis-fying breakfast of scrambled eggs with cheddar cheese, bacon and a biscuit with jam. Lilly makes fabulous buttermilk biscuits with a maple bourbon glaze. When Karen is not with me, I tend to in-dulge a bit. Karen wasn't with me because she was in class.

It was great that she wanted to be a lawyer. Being around a great lawyer tends to inspire that in people. Karen was as smart as a whip and had a logical mind. Of course, having been my close companion, she had been exposed to the moves of a master. She was going to be spectacular.

But, I missed her. Among other things it meant that I was going to have breakfast alone four days a week. I realize I needed exer-cise, so it was okay that she had the Jaguar. The six blocks downhill to our house made me feel virtuous. I always try to keep up a fast pace. My pace today was even faster than normal because it was raining again. I use "again" loosely. Yes, it was the rainy season, but this was ridiculous.

You might say I have mixed feelings about all this. On the good side, I really don't like poached eggs and dry toast. Karen thought, wrongly I might add, that I could become sleeker. She has devel-oped this annoying habit of pinching my very small love handles and going "hmmm."

On the bad side, she is always good company. And she's sexy as hell. She makes me look good, not, of course, that that it is necessary. My smile had been known to drive virgins wild and to cause women drivers to stop in the middle of the road and stare. I try not to smile too much when I am out-of-doors. I dislike chaos.

Rain deadens the sound and had closed me into the little private world of my thoughts. I was a bit distracted thinking about Laura Evenwell's interview after our announcement. That had gone well. There were several telephone calls that evening from friends and acquaintances. People really seemed to have gotten into the joke. It was going to be a shame to give it up.

The rain water was sweeping down the street and our little creek was overflowing. The rain wasn't exactly falling in buckets, but it was a steady, cold rain. If this went on, I might have to buy water wings. It might be an opportune time to see how our neighbors were coming along with the ark. My only concern, of course, was for Karen and Bruno, but you can't be too careful.

I was my usual natty self, dressed in pressed jeans and my nifty cowboy shirt with the pearl buttons. I had on my second-best Stetson and a really nice raincoat that I had buttoned up to my neck. My cold was almost gone.

My umbrella had been selected this morning to match my ensemble. I had it angled over my shoulder. The wind was pushing the rain from behind me. The umbrella was doing a moderately adequate job of keeping me dry.

I'm a resilient kind of guy however so I was holding up pretty well. You know, the happy kind who everyone wants to be around. I was singing to myself. I do that all the time. It is quite nice.

Several of my friends have observed that I should consider a professional singing career. They suggested that a lot of people would pay me not to sing. Some of my friends don't have the ear for music with which I am blessed.

I couldn't see anything behind me. My head was down and I was looking where I stepped. There were mud puddles everywhere.

I was hunched beneath my umbrella and it was blocking my view. But I became aware of a car coming down the street. He was driving too fast. I turned to look as he passed me. The car swerved towards the curb. Had the idiot lost control. I stopped walking and stepped several steps back from the street.

The sharp turn created a wave of water in the flooded street. The water peaked and came down over me. I was soaked to the skin. Even through my raincoat. My socks were wet. I think my best lizard skin boots drowned. I knew I should have worn my old Justin boots.

My pants were wet. My shirt was wet. The only thing that was modestly dry was my raincoat. Of course.

I was not pleased. I may have said "darn." I may have even said "shucks." I certainly was shivering.

The car, one of those big Chevys, braked sharply to a halt about 6 feet from me, sending another wave over the curb onto my boots and trouser legs. This idiot better apologize. He rolled down the window. Rain was splashing on his arm. He didn't seem to care.

The guy in the driver's seat looked familiar. I have a great memory for faces, particularly when they are attached to someone who beat me up. Gino Bartoletti's thug, the Fire Plug, sat there, baring his teeth in a smile that he stole from a ratty tiger.

Gino Bartoletti had been the head of the United Union Pension fund and was identified by the FBI as a known associate of the Gambrella crime family. He was not a nice man. Mr. Bartoletti apparently felt that I had not been paying sufficient attention to his desires and he expressed his displeasure by sending the Fire Plug to visit me one evening. We enjoyed a spirited discussion in which the Fire Plug delivered Mr. Bartoletti's message severely. The Fire Plug enjoyed our chat. I didn't. I still have sore spots.

I wince at the memory. I remember it well. "Mr. Bartoletti don't think you understand him too good. He thinks you got a smart mouth. I explain it to you." Then he hit me and kicked me in the ribs, more than once. I'm a quick learner.

Mr. Bartoletti was the undisclosed financier of the Franklin Farms, an upscale housing development by Mr. Guy Mason. He was also the boyfriend of my client, Janet Mason, the star of the series *Desperate Shop Girls*. As you may have guessed, Mr. Mason was the husband of my client. Unfortunately, both Mr. and Ms. Mason came to a bad end, marking one of my more unpleasant visits with our then Chief of Police, now mayoral candidate, Walter Carsone.

So, as you can imagine, I was not pleased to renew my acquaintance with the Fire Plug. I don't think he liked me.

"Hey, asshole," he said, motioning me over with his finger. "Come here."

I thought about running. The sidewalks in our little town only run along Main Street. Elsewhere, we usually walk on the little trodden paths that run alongside the road. The water in the street was moving quickly, hoping over the curb in places. The ground around me was so muddy I would sink in if I tried to run. And he had a car. I took a cautious step towards him.

"What the fuck do ya think you're doing." He didn't look happy. I was very concerned about his happiness.

I knew what I was doing. I was dripping like a leaky faucet. I could have told him that. But I don't think it's what he meant. I didn't shrivel. At least not where anyone could see. I may have looked around desperately over both shoulders to see if there was anyone who would help. But that's only wise, isn't it. There were none however. Most people are too smart to be out walking in a heavy rain.

I shook my head sharply, shedding water like a wet puppy. "Wha… What do you mean?"

"With this dog shit."

Well, that was out of context.

What was Fire Plug doing here? The Fed's had suggested to Mr. Bartoletti after the Franklin Farms affair that they would be happy if he cooperated with their inquiries and that he might consider not spending the rest of his life in jail. Then they had made him disappear. Along with the Fire Plug.

In my opinion, they made the wrong decision, but they didn't ask me for my advice. I think he was the guy who murdered Janet Mason.

Why was the Fire Plug busting me about Bruno? Was Gino Bartoletti involved? They weren't comforting questions.

Mr. Bartoletti hadn't been heard of in years. I didn't miss him. But now I was looking straight at his goon.

"You mean about Bruno running for mayor?" I asked. My voice was the soul of innocence. To my credit, I didn't stammer. I may have squeaked.

"Yeah, that shit," The Fire Plug said. I don't think this man can talk without a snarl.

"That's just a joke." It is true my voice might have risen. I certainly don't believe it could be described as pleading. I wasn't going to be able to stand here much longer without drowning.

"Well, Mr. Carsone ain't got no sense of humor."

Golly, that was a surprise.

"You remember me, right," he said.

I shook my head up and down in an emphatic "yes." I had to stop doing that, or I was going to drown. I had forgotten about my umbrella. I was holding it down at my side.

Worse, the wind had shifted and the rain was blowing into my face. It was making its way down my neck inside my raincoat. I was still shivering. No not from fear. At least, not only from fear.

I was thinking rapidly. The Fire Plug must have been the guy who scared Allie Niddle.

"You remember what happened last time, don't ya." He stared at me and laughed. I didn't find it funny.

I shook my head up and down again. Damn.

A wave of water hopped the curve and ran over the toe of my boot. I looked down and shifted back a step. But the Fire Plug's voice caught and held my attention.

"Look at me, asshole."

I complied. Not willingly. I just wanted to be polite.

"Mr. Carsone don't want no more of this shit or someone's gonna get hurt. Bad."

He rolled up his window and hit the gas, sending another wave of water over my boots.

Chapter 19

I MADE QUITE A splash when I got to the office. Clyde was in the reception room. Pamela was nowhere to be found, of course. He took one look at me and went into the bathroom to grab a towel. He handed it to me. I dried my hair.

"Massah, has you been out swimming in yo clothes again? I done told you it be bad. Why you go and done it?" I ignored him.

He helped me out of my raincoat. I felt exhausted. I could hardly hold up my head.

"Clyde, do you remember the Fire Plug? Gino Bartoletti's thug," I managed to get out a little breathlessly.

"Sure do," Clyde said. "Bad dude."

"I just ran into him or visa versa. We have another problem."

"Go up and change into some dry clothes. You look better dry." Clyde said, reverting to his best English.

"You're right. I'll change and tell you what happened. I think we may have to do something about Bruno's campaign sooner rather than later."

"Good. Say hello to Paolo on your way by. He's been here since early morning cooking for tonight."

I had completely forgotten about the dinner with Gilbert Sachs.

Gilbert Sachs turned out to be different than I had imagined a food critic would be. He was tall and thin. He had a long face and a prominent nose. And he had a graying beard. He was neat, but not particularly well dressed. He was clearly bright and seemed friendly.

Paolo greeted him fulsomely.

"Meester Sachs, I am Paolo Marino. I am pleased to meet so famoose a man. I read alla your reviews." Fortunately, Paolo didn't kiss him. That might have gotten the evening off to a rocky start.

The smells drifting in from the kitchen made my mouth water. The mixed aromas of spices and meats was exquisite. I could even smell them through my stuffy nose.

Gilbert Sachs and Paolo were immediately on a first name basis. With Paolo, anything else was basically impossible. He looked splendid in chef's whites. The buttons tugged across his stomach in a prosperous sort of way. His name was stitched on his chest. He didn't have on one of those tall white hats, thank goodness.

"Geelbert," he said, "may I introduce my friends?" We were all gathered expectantly at the end of the conference table that was now set for dinner. Paolo hadn't touched the walls of the room, which surprised me. All of the posters of Bruno were still there.

He made an open-handed gesture to Karen. "Thess beautiful lady es Karen Harris. She es not only beautifool, which is wunderful thing, but also, she is brilliant. She study to be a lawyer." Karen looked exquisite in the blue dress she keeps for special occasions.

Gilbert Sachs took Karen's hand and kissed it. I was jealous. But I restrained myself.

How Paolo had found linens and crystal for the table was beyond me, but the conference room looked more elegant than I had ever seen it. There were sterling silver place settings. Even with the posters on the wall, it sparkled.

But that was nothing compared to seeing the presence of our Pamela, all dressed up and passing little rounds of toast topped with beautiful minced crab, garnished with tiny flowers. I mean, he got Pamela to show up and actually do something useful. I'd have to ask him for his secret.

"And please you meet Clyde Budan. I pronounce that correctly, Clyde? It es hard for me, this English."

"You did great Paolo, it's a Jamaican name, not English," Clyde said, extending his hand to Gilbert Sachs. They shook.

Clyde had on a blue blazer over gray slacks. Under the blazer he had on a high necked dark gray cashmere sweater. The outfit was set off by a red pocket handkerchief.

Paolo, continued. "Clyde is law partner of Jemmy. Very fine lawyer."

Then Paolo turned to me. "And this is Jemmy Harris. He is my lawyer. Famoose, like you."

I had dried out and pretty much quit shaking. I wasn't at my best, but I was presentable.

"Pleased to meet you, Mr. Harris," Sachs, said, turning towards me and stepping forward, his hand extended. I shook it.

"Finally, Geelbert, you meet Bruno." He pointed down at Bruno's uplifted face. Bruno had his tongue hanging out. He was fully dressed with a scarf around his neck in the red, white and green colors of Italy. He looked quite distinguished. "He most intelligent dog. Very popular in San Buenasara."

To my surprise, Sachs got down on one knee. Bruno lifted his paw. He was becoming adept at it. Sachs took it solemnly. "It's nice to meet you, Bruno." Then he scratched Bruno behind the ears. "He's beautiful," Sachs enthused. "A long-haired dachshund?" he asked quizzically, looking up at me while he rubbed Bruno's back.

"Yes," I said. Always succinct.

Paolo quietly slipped from the conference room into the kitchen.

"I had a dachshund when I was a kid. I loved that dog. I love this dog." Sachs had a big smile on his face.

Given how Bruno was wagging his tail, the feeling was mutual.

Sachs noticed the posters on the wall. His smile turned curious. He got to his feet, walked over and looked closely at one. Then he moved sideways and looked at a second one.

"This is unusual," he said focusing on another one of the posters. "Is Bruno really running for mayor?"

"It's a joke, Gilbert. We didn't like the other candidate, so we nominated Bruno. We had his announcement rally two nights ago. It was quite a party."

Sachs was chuckling and shaking his head as Paolo came back into the conference room holding a bottle of 2014 Benoit Dehu champagne. Paolo set it on the table.

"I lika small champagne house, Geelbert. You find this good maybe."

Then Paolo unwrapped the foil and twisted off the wire holding the cork. With a deft turn of his wrist, he withdrew the cork with a pop. I surmised he had done this before. There were champagne flutes on the table. Paolo poured the champagne himself.

I guess it's not like beer because Paolo poured it straight into the glass and let the bubbles cream at the top. I don't know anything about champagne, but given the look of attention on Gilbert Sachs' face, I was impressed.

I don't drink, but I had Perrier in a champagne flute. I fit right in.

Paolo held up his flute. "Salute," he said brightly. We echoed the word as we clicked glasses.

"How did you hear about Paolo?" I asked, turning to Sachs.

"Jimmy, Paolo's restaurant in Italy is one of the most famous in the world. I've known of Paolo for years. I ate there once, but Paolo was away on a trip. His food was superb, but I never got to meet him. I was in Los Angeles and one of my sources told me Paolo was here to open a restaurant. I couldn't miss the chance to meet him and taste his food again."

"Well, we're glad you came."

"Please, you taka your seat," Paolo said making a sweeping hand gesture. He motioned Gilbert to the seat at the head of the table. "Please, Geelbert, you sit here. We sit Karen on your right."

The rest of us sat down too. I was next to Gilbert, across from Karen. Paolo sat at the other end of the table. Clyde was between Karen and Paolo. We made Bruno sit on the floor. He gave me a dour look.

Then the first course arrived. Paolo had hired Mario, the owner of our local Italian restaurant to assist as his sous chef. Mario's wife served the food. She was dressed in black and looked great.

The first course was superb. Then there were small cups of a tart lemon sorbet. And after that came the Steak Florentine, which was so tender it simply melted in my mouth. It was delicious. We had salad at the end. But the hit of the evening was dessert.

Paolo had baked Italian Wedding Cookies in the shape of dog biscuits again. But these were iced with a portrait of Bruno. It was a work of art, done with just a few lines of icing. He served it with a rich, handmade vanilla ice cream.

Paolo was not only a great chef. He was a showman. He served dessert with a flourish.

Bruno slept under the table lying across Gilbert Sachs' feet. That boy had made a new friend. So had Paolo.

Chapter 20

WE COULDN'T GET TOGETHER until very late the next afternoon. Karen had classes and Clyde had to appear at an afternoon hearing. Some matter that had to do with a claim that the city's lack of maintenance on the streets had caused an accident. At the rate our city was going with street maintenance, San Buenasara would be the first city to fall into the ocean as the result of a giant pothole.

I personally looked upon our city's decisions as a safety measure. After all, if you couldn't drive more than 20 miles an hour, how could you have an accident? It had the additional benefit of lowering traffic injuries. Pedestrians could fall asleep while crossing the street and still wake up in time to avoid being run over.

It had been a long, but happy night with Paolo and Gilbert Sachs, so I slept in. Sachs promised that he would have his review into the editors of the *Times* by morning, although he warned Paolo that it was up to his editors when it would be published.

Clyde, Karen and I really had to discuss how we were going to announce Bruno's withdrawal from the mayor's race before someone got hurt. Our joke had come off a little too well.

At about 2 o'clock Clyde rolled in from court. His hearing had apparently gone well. He was whistling and seemed upbeat. He poked his head into the conference room. Karen wasn't back from San Luis, so Clyde went into his office.

She came into the conference room around 2:45, kissed me

and put her briefcase on the floor. She pulled out a chair and sat down.

"Busy day," she said, giving her head a little shake. I called out Clyde's name.

Pamela was on a break.

The conference room was now spotless. Paolo had arranged for it to be cleaned this morning. I had glanced into the kitchen. It hadn't looked so good in months. It rarely needed to be cleaned. More like dusted.

Clyde was still in his courthouse armor. Dark blue suit with a subtle maroon stripe. He had on a starched blue custom-made shirt, with a green silk tie, patterned to accent the color of the stripe in his suit. That boy does know how to dress. Maybe we were paying him too much. He was carrying a cup of coffee.

Clyde took the chair across from me and put the cup of coffee down on the table. He started turning it absently in his hands.

Karen was in blue jeans and a red cotton cowboy shirt. Karen has the kind of figure that looks good in whatever she is wearing. I've told her many times since we met that she didn't have to wear anything for me, but she still does, darn it.

The sun had actually come out and light was dancing on the conference room table, almost as if it was delighted to join the party. I had put out soft drinks and water but everyone ignored them.

I was in jeans too, but then, I look well turned out in anything.

We settled in. Karen looked at me expectantly. After all, I am the senior partner. Then she turned to Clyde.

"What do you think?" she asked. Hey, what about me?

"I've got to tell you, I have mixed feelings," Clyde said, his voice having a tentative edge. He stopped turning the coffee cup. "I don't like the way Carsone is trying to steamroller us."

That was a terrible pun, but I don't think Clyde noticed. His mind didn't work that way. Others did. Clyde paused thoughtfully.

"I'm worried that Gino Bartoletti's goon has reappeared," I interrupted.

"We all are," Clyde said. So far, Karen was just listening, but she had her jaw set and she was opening and closing her hands.

"Why is the goon working for Carsone? And is Bartoletti involved?" I continued. "We know he's a bad guy who doesn't mind hurting people."

"This is what I was afraid of," Karen interjected. "I don't think there's any way we can protect ourselves and still keep Bruno in the race." I hate it when Karen is right.

"I agree," Clyde said. "Maybe if the FBI was involved. Local police are not going to help, that's for sure. Perhaps the FBI would be interested in what Bartoletti is doing? They put him in witness protection. But I think that's a real longshot."

"Do you think the state police would intervene? After all, it is an election." I like the way my mind works.

"Maybe, Jimmy," Clyde said. "But I don't think they have jurisdiction. It's a pretty local matter. Could be that the Sheriff would get involved, but I don't see that we have enough evidence to get her attention. We would have to explain to them that you were all wet."

Clyde turned deliberately towards me and gave me a toothy smile. I think he was just trying to break the tension. Karen giggled.

How sharper than a serpent's tooth.

"You think we have to bite the bullet," I said with reluctance.

"Yeah, but we gotta make sure the bullet is pointing out if we're going to bite it," Clyde added. The image in my mind made me wince. But, it struck me as sage advice.

"I don't like to give up. It feels cowardly. But I think we have to be really careful. It isn't worth anyone getting hurt," Karen said.

"Clyde, do you want to write a press release?" I asked.

"I can call Linda Evenwell and explain why Bruno is withdrawing," I continued.

"What are you going to tell her, Jimmy?"

"I haven't figured that out yet."

As it turned out, I didn't have to. There was a knock on the door and an excited Paolo Marino put his head into the room. He was holding a newspaper.

"You see this," he said, shaking the paper at us. "It'sa wunderful." He was practically dancing.

And it was great. Or maybe terrible. It certainly changed everything we were thinking.

Chapter 21

"GILBERT SACHS, HE WRITE wunderful review. Good for Bruno too," Paolo said holding out the paper to me. It was folded to the restaurant reviews.

"That's great Paolo," I said, confused, taking the paper from him. I started to read the review but Karen stopped me.

"Jimmy, why don't you read it out loud."

I did. Who said I don't take instruction well.

As a food critic, I have been all over the world and have had many unusual experiences. Some have been wonderful, some otherwise.

Last Thursday was one of those unusual experiences. This one may top them all.

I was in a little town called San Buenasara, up the coast of California, a little south of San Luis Obispo. That's more or less half way between San Francisco and Los Angeles. I was in San Buenasara because I heard that one of my favorite chefs, Paolo Marino, was there and thinking about opening a restaurant.

Now, I don't usually review a restaurant before it is open. But, as I have said many times in my column, Italy is my favorite restaurant. Paolo has a little restaurant in Pienza, a little village, in Tuscany from which he turns out divine food. He has two well deserved Michlin stars and deserves a third. The chance to eat his cooking again was irresistible and I wanted to see why he was in a

98

little town in California and what he was thinking.

Paolo interrupted. "You see," Paolo made a broad gesture with his hand. He write wunderful review." Everyone agreed cheerfully as I continued.

Believe me when I say San Buenasara is rustic. The best restaurant in town is a coffee shop with a frog décor. The heart of the shopping district, which is about three blocks long, is Pussy Galore, an adult toy store. I can't imagine what the folks do at night for entertainment. I don't think I want to know."

Now I thought that was a bit unfair. I think inquiring minds always want to know.

I was welcomed by Paolo into a cute little two-story cottage. He introduced me to his friends, a nice couple and a tall, distinguished looking, young lawyer. There was a dog, a long-haired dachshund, wearing a scarf around his neck in the colors of Italy. The dog and I shook hands. He is quite a fellow.

Paolo cooks simple food exquisitely. We ate in what looked like a conference room. I was told that our hosts were lawyers and this was their office. That was strange because there were campaign posters all over the walls.

The surroundings might have been unusual, but the food was exquisite. Every bit as good as I remembered. Perhaps better. The flavors of Paolo Marino's cooking burst like fireworks on your tongue.

I stopped, remembering my manners. "Paolo, can we get you something to drink?"

"No, Jemmy, I am too fine. You read some more.

Paolo prepared Bistecca alla Fiorintina, simple steak rubbed in olive oil, salt and some spices Paolo refused to disclose. It is always served rare, or in Italian, "Al sangue." You can be banned from Tuscany ordering it any other way. I don't know where Paolo got his beef, but this melted in your mouth. He preceded the steak with tagliatelle Bolognese, again simple, but somehow totally his own.

"Gilbert Sachs, he love my food," Paolo interrupted. "You like my food too, Jemmy?'

Karen shifted in her chair as she answered for all of us.

"Paolo, we all love your food. I was a real treat for us. Thank you."

I read on.

Paolo served it with a 2015 Ciacci Piccolomini d'Aragona Brunello di Montalcino. That is one of the finest Brunello's from a great year. It was beautifully aged. I have no idea how Paolo found it. It was a perfect accompaniment to the steak once the wine had rested in the glass to allow the tannins to resolve.

I personally prefer a Brunello to a Super Tuscan. Super Tuscans can be made with Cabernet Sauvignon grapes. Just fine with meats, of course. But I find the Brunellos, made from Sangiovese, tighter and more perfumed.

However, the highlight of the meal was dessert, Italian Wedding Cookies. But that is where it all got, I would say unusual. I think that may be an understatement. These cookies were shaped like large dog biscuits, not the normal small balls topped with candy confetti. There was a dachshund on top, done masterfully in icing.

When I asked about it, everyone around the table laughed. I laughed too, although I didn't know why I was laughing.

Paolo pointed at Bruno, the dog.

There was a bit of dramatic license here, but since it was a food review, I permitted it.

"He ess Bruno. He is running for mayor of San Buenasara. I do these for him. They are very good, yes?"

Well, yes, but not as good as the story of a dog who is running for mayor. I would tell you that story, but my colleague, Ronald

Jalewsky, the political reporter for the New York Times, *threatened me with horrible punishment if I gave away any of the story he intends to write. He threatened to make me eat at McDonald's for the rest of my life. And drink only Diet Coke.*

So, keep an eye out.

I laid the paper on the table and got up.

"Paolo, this is great for you. I'm glad," I said leaning over and slapping him on the back.

"See, is good, no. For all of us."

My mind froze as I tried to parse that sentence. I wasn't so sure it was great for Bruno or for any of us, but it certainly changed things. And Sachs said there was going to be another article.

Maybe we should consider hiring armed guards. Or perhaps an army.

Chapter 22

NOTHING HAPPENED FOR THREE days. Except that I kept looking over my shoulder and jumping at any unexpected noise. We had gone quiet with Bruno's campaign. There was no sense in poking the bear. The bear seemed to be hibernating.

There was no indication that Carsone or any of his people had read the *New York Times* restaurant review. There was no indication any of them could read.

Carsone had a campaign rally yesterday. He drew about 20 people. The *San Buenasara Journal* reported it as an overwhelming success.

On the third day after Gilbert Sachs' article, the *New York Times* published the follow-up. We had no need for Paolo to alert us to its publication. We had been reading the *Times* every day, waiting for the other shoe to drop. It did, with a thud.

Clyde was the first to discover the article. Karen and I gathered in Clyde's office. We were perched on his two client chairs.

It had started to rain again. Perhaps it was prophetic. He started reading.

Dogging It by Ronald Jalewsky
   Writing about political matters is a serious endeavor. Politics are important. But on rare occasions, it simply cannot sustain a completely serious tone. Notwithstanding that, the matters addressed are vital indeed.

The mayoral election in the small California town of San Bue-
nasara is capturing the attention of the nation. Our Research De-
partment has been unable to identify any other modern election in
which a man is running against a dog.

Our editorial staff asked: "Why is a dog running?" They are
people of deep insights and few words.

When we published the restaurant review that disclosed this
unusual election in the Central California city of San Buenasara,
there was a lot of laughter among my colleagues. But surprisingly,
there was an unprecedented outpouring from our readers. Perhaps
we all need a little relief from all that is going wrong today in our
country and in the world.

I was intrigued, but I was prepared for the moment to pursue
other, more important stories, like our messy national election, the
wars that were ripping us apart or the rise of fascism throughout
the world.

My editor, however, expressed to me his concern with my pro-
posed choices, and his desire, none too subtlety framed, that I imme-
diately follow up on the San Buenasara article.

I determined to investigate. To my surprise, my editor actually
gave me a budget.

I concluded that an election poll would be illuminating. After
consulting with my colleagues, I contacted the University of Chi-
cago. The University of Chicago agreed to partner with the New
York Times *to conduct a poll. At least I believe they agreed. It was*
hard to tell because the person on the other end of the line could
hardly catch her breath, she was laughing so hard.

Our poll was based upon a random sampling of 382 registered
voters in San Buenasara, selected at random and contacted by tele-
phone over a two-day period.

"I had no idea there were 382 registered voters in San Buenasara, at least ones who were awake," I said, interrupting.

"Jimmy, just listen," Clyde said rather acerbically. Karen nodded
briskly in agreement.

Bruno was lying on the new, high-backed leather chair we dragged in from the conference room. He seemed to like it. He won't let me sit in it. I didn't think he was paying enough attention to the article. He was focused on licking his balls. It was embarrassing.

Clyde continued to read from the *Times*.

We asked six questions, carefully constructed by the University to be non-partisan and unbiased. Participants were given the opportunity to express their views without disclosing their identities.

306 voters answered our call. 285 didn't hang up or call us names.

Of the 285 respondents, 37% identified as Republicans, 48% as Democrats and 15% suggested we perform an impossible anatomical act. The answers, based upon our interviews show that 58% of the voters of San Buenasara will vote for the dog, 26% for the former Chief of Police, Walter 'Wally' Carsone, and 16% were undecided.

These results naturally led to other questions. We believe that the attitude in San Buenasara, reflected in this poll, is attributable to a more basic question. Can a dog be perceived as more trustworthy and more discerning than a politician in the view of the electorate. That answer appears to be unequivocally "yes," not only based upon this poll, but upon other current political races.

This may represent a major shift in public sentiment and an attitude transcendent in the current political environment. For example, in the recent race for Governor of Arkansas, 42% of the voters wrote in on their ballots, "Who the f… cares." The remainder of the ballots appear to have been marked with large x's, written in crayon, for one candidate or the other.

Republicans in Arkansas immediately claimed, before the vote was counted, that it represented an overwhelming endorsement of their policies. The Democrats seem to have been focused on the national policy implications of the misspelling of the word 'f…' on many of the write – in ballots.

The New York Times *promises we will follow this story. It*

*may change politics as we know it. Our hope is to get to know the
candidates, their strengths and weaknesses. To learn what motivates
them and their constituents. And to bring you the outcome of this
herculean struggle. Will San Buenasara go to the dogs?*

"I never expected that anyone would do a poll in San Buenasara," I said. "Carsone must be furious. This makes him look like
an idiot," I said.

"And your point?" Clyde observed.

"Do you think Carsone will notice the article?" I asked.

"If he doesn't, someone else will. Someone like Laura Evenwell.
I expect Mr. Carsone may be getting a call." Clyde ventured.

"Do you actually think Bruno can win?" Karen asked.

"I think the more important question is whether Carsone or
maybe Bartolettii thinks he can win. They have a lot of money in-
vested in this campaign. And I'm certain of one thing. The people
doing the investing are not nice people," I sagely observed.

"You're scaring me," Karen said. She shifted in her seat and
clasped her hands in her lap.

"Good, I'm scaring myself."

"You can count me in on that, Boss. We have an issue."

"What do you think we should do?" Karen asked.

As I opened my mouth to respond, the conference room door
opened and Pamela's stuck her head around the edge. I closed
my mouth.

"Jimmy, there's a call for you."

I turned in my seat to look at her. There was a strange look on
her face.

"Not now, Pamela. We're dealing with something important." I
can be commanding.

"You have to take it." There was no question in her voice. So
much for commanding.

"Why?"

"He says it's Scott Pelley from *60 Minutes*. They want to do a
segment on Bruno and the election."

The cat was out of the bag. The horse was out of the barn. Karen looked at me.

"We can't announce Bruno's withdrawal now, can we?" she said.

"I don't think it will do any good. This is going to drive Carsone nuts," Clyde interjected.

"If we can't get out, we need to do everything we can to get Bruno elected," I said with authority of my role as campaign manager. "The more publicity we get, the less likely Carsone and his backers are to attempt anything. There would be a firestorm and they have to want to avoid that." I hope.

"So, we do a real campaign, starting now?" Clyde asked.

Karen shrugged. "I don't see any other way."

Chapter 23

IT HAD BEEN TWO days since the article appeared in the *New York Times* under the title "Dogging It." I thought the article was really funny. I thought the idea of San Buenasara going to the dogs was great. Maybe not if you were Chief Carsone.

The article promised a follow-up investigation and assured its readers that they would come to know these two candidates well.

It did not mention that Bruno was charming and appeared to have exceptional gravitas, as well as enthusiastic local backing. When I arrived at the office, Pamela was actually there. Her desk was piled with mail. There was a pile of checks next to the corner of her desk, some opened letters and three piles of unopened mail. She was shaking her head.

"Golly," she said, "we've received $800 in donations to Bruno's campaign just from the letters I've opened."

"That's great. We can use the money." Maybe we wouldn't go bankrupt mounting this campaign.

"There are also two death threats and three antisemitic letters."

"Bruno's not Jewish." I'm observant. You have to be to be a great lawyer.

"I guess some people can't tell," Pamela observed.

"There are also three marriage proposals. One came with a nude photograph," she said with a whisper of wonder in her voice.

"Can I see it?" I held out my hand eagerly.

"No," Karen said from behind me, walking into the reception room from her own small office, stepping around me and taking the picture from Pamela's outstretched hand.

"You're too young." She slapped my hand and smiled. But she didn't let me see the photograph. I mean, I just wanted to see the kind of woman who would want to marry Bruno.

It was obvious to me that some people don't know who's boss here. Actually, no one does. I just sulked.

I picked up the stack of checks and thumbed through them. The largest was for $50. In the note section at the bottom, the sender had written "It was the dog that did it." That would be a great opening line for a book, I thought. Then I brushed the thought away. There were more important issues.

Karen picked up the checks and handed them to me.

"You're the campaign manager. Go open a bank account and deposit them." Then she turned and walked back into her office. She took the photograph with her.

I folded the checks in half and tucked them into my breast pocket of my nifty cowboy shirt and snapped the pearl button shut. I would have to stop by the bank and deposit the money.

I wondered whether there was a way to continue the publicity. It was wonderful what a little notoriety could do. Eight hundred dollars and three marriage proposals weren't a bad start. And who knew what might follow.

Maybe I should call the reporter for the *New York Times*. Perhaps some of the other papers would pick up the story.

It was a good story. Can a dog be a good mayor? Would he be better than some people? This was a deep philosophical issue. I could see a world of interest. Maybe even social media. Who was young enough around here to tell me how that works?

I would have to think of hiring a six-year-old for our campaign staff. These were the kinds of decisions that could make or break a campaign.

Then I focused on the death threats. We'd have to take those seriously, and I didn't think going to the local police was going to help. I needed to discuss this with Clyde and Karen, sooner rather than later.

Pamela's comment brought me back from my thoughts.

"Who would threaten to kill a sweet puppy? What kind of idiots are out there?"

"There are some politicians I could understand killing," I asserted. Kidding, of course.

Bruno was hardly a puppy, but he was sweet, at least to Karen. And he hadn't let all the attention go to his head. He was no less pleased with himself than he had ever been. And people had taken to bringing him dog biscuits. Anyone who knows Bruno knows that he treasures treats, even if they are his just deserts. We needed to give some thoughts as to how to protect him. Just in case.

Bruno is self-confident. He wouldn't let the adulation of a campaign go to his head, would he?

I hoped Bruno would talk to me after this was all over. I mean, not that he talked to me a lot as it was.

Chapter 24

"LOOK AT ALL THESE people. There must be over 80," I said. Karen and I were standing to the side of the Lilly Pad's main dining room. I was leaning in close to her ear. The room was filled with chatter. Lots of people were milling around.

"This is kind of unbelievable," Karen said, surveying the crowd. There was a noticeable rise in her voice.

"Yeah, unbelievable. All these people turned out in this kind of weather to support Bruno."

Bruno was still in the back room. The groomer was putting the finishing touches on him. A candidate has to look his best.

Polly was wandering through the crowd. He was smiling and shaking hands with people. He looked our way and came over.

"I'm glad I'm on Bruno's ticket. This is quite a crowd." Someone tapped him on the shoulder and he turned and wandered off into a discussion with several folks.

Maybe it wasn't such a good idea to have our first campaign rally at the Lilly Pad.

However, there wasn't much choice. It was the only place in town that was big enough. At least for free. When you are mounting a campaign with our resources, the word "free" is exciting.

Lilly had offered to close early. "Come on, Jimmy, I support my customers. And Bruno and Karen are the best."

Those were her exact words. I knew something was missing

there, but I couldn't put my finger on it.

It was around 8 o'clock. Lilly had pushed the tables aside to create a large open room. It was raining like hell. The room smelled of wet wool and damp people. We had arrived an hour early, when the rain was still just a sprinkle. It had gotten its wind up since then.

The beer was flowing like our creek and some of the young law students were constantly replacing plates of Bruno cookies.

It was hard to believe Bruno was this popular. It could be that people just liked the cookies. Maybe we had touched something deep in the feelings of our neighbors. Maybe they were as scared of Carsone as we were.

Paolo was up day and night baking more cookies. He said they kept disappearing. I thought I could see where they were disappearing to. Unfortunately, so could Karen. I wish she would quit poking around.

But it can't be just the cookies. People were actually waving homemade signs.

A woman over on the left held hers up. "Dog It," it said in big black letters outlined in red.

I liked that. I thought we should use that on our website.

What website? The one Clyde is going to set up tomorrow.

Right.

I turned to Karen. She had a quizzical look on her face as she turned her head towards me.

"Can people really want to elect Bruno?"

"I have no idea what is going on," I said with certainty.

"Take a look at that." Karen pointed towards the front door.

Bruno had made his appearance and was now working the room. Everyone wanted to pet him. They crowded around him as he wandered from person to person. What great political instincts. And he liked to be petted.

He was holding up his paw to shake hands with Polly. "I think he's a natural born ham," Karen said with a giggle. She put her hand on my arm as she laughed.

"Don't tell him," I said. "He thinks he's a dog. We don't want to confuse him."

Maybe people really hate Carsone. That's not hard to believe.

It's kind of heartening when you think about it. Maybe these people really care about their little town. Maybe they don't want it to change.

"Do you think Bruno is going to become insufferable if he becomes Mayor?"

"He does love attention," Karen said.

"But we're his family," I pointed out.

"He'll probably let us pet him," Karen pronounced. She put her lips together and gave an emphatic nod.

I knew Bruno would let Karen pet him. He might let me pet him too, if I was lucky.

Chapter 25

My phone rang. I picked it up and punched in.

"Jimmy, help me," Karen said. Her voice was shrill and frightened.

I sat up straight in my chair. I was in the office, working on the next rally for Bruno.

"Karen, what's wrong? Are you hurt?"

"No, I'm not hurt."

"Thank God!" I said it with the exclamation point showing.

"But I'm scared to death. Please help me." It was almost a shriek.

"Where are you?"

"I'm in the parking garage next to the law school. I'm kneeling down behind the car." Karen had been driving the Jaguar to class.

"Are you in danger."

"Jimmy, I don't know." Her voice was ragged at the edges.

"What happened?"

"I came out of class and went to get in the car. Two of the tires have been cut and there's an ice pick sticking up out of the front fender."

"Is there anyone else around?"

"No, the garage is deserted." I could almost feel her looking around, terrified.

"I'll borrow Clyde's car and be right there. Do you have the number of the law school on your phone?"

"Yes."

"Good, call the dean's office and ask him to send someone from Security to walk you back to school. Tell him what happened. Then call me back and I'll stay on the line with you until someone comes."

"Okay. Jimmy, this is so frightening."

"I know, honey. Let's get you safe."

Karen hung up. I was clenching my teeth hard. I could feel the pressure from my jaw in my temples. Karen was one of the calmest, bravest people I knew. I also didn't know what I would do without her. What a thought. I just sat there and clutched my cell phone. My knuckles were white. The phone rang less than a minute later.

"The dean said he will come himself as well as bringing someone from Security. He said it would be two minutes." She still sounded shaky.

But I think I breathed for the first time since we hung up.

"Okay, stay with me." My body wouldn't relax. "Do you hear any sounds?"

"Now there are some kids laughing on the next floor down."

"That's good. There are other people around. Did you notice anyone following you?"

"Not in person."

"I don't understand."

"I felt like someone was following me when I drove to school this morning. I kept seeing this big black car, off and on, behind me."

Big black car.

"Do you think it followed you from the house."

"Jimmy, I don't know."

I heard her shout, "Up here." Her voice was muffled. She must have been holding the phone away from her mouth. And then I heard other faint voices. Karen said, "Thank you, Dean Matthews, for coming so quickly."

I couldn't hear what Dean Matthews said in reply. But Karen said, "That will be nice. I'll feel safe in your office. This is horrible."

Apparently, Matthews responded, because I heard an indistinct voice in the background. I couldn't make out the words.

Karen came back on the phone." Jimmy, I'm going to the Dean's office."

"That's great, darling. I'll borrow Clyde's car or rent one. I'll be there in 30 minutes. Then I'll take you home."

"Oh, Jimmy, what are we going to do with the Jaguar, the poor thing."

The Jaguar had certainly taken its share of abuse in the last two years. It had been knifed, cut up and shot in the motor. I remember how sad it was, seeing the Jaguar clawing at the sides of the flat-bed tow truck hauling it away for a heart transplant.

Now it had been ice-picked. I wouldn't be surprised if it was thinking about quitting. I know I would.

"Don't worry, honey. I'll call the Auto Club and have it towed to Billy's." Billy was our new mechanic. I think he loves the Jaguar almost as much as we do. God knows, he sees enough of her.

"I guess we'll have to rent a car."

"Not to worry. I've got it covered. Now let me get there. I love you."

I was off to beg the car from Clyde. I didn't like the sound of that big black car at all.

When I got up, Bruno stood up too. Bruno doesn't stand up very high, but he's a stand-up guy whenever Karen needs him.

"You heard that, big guy. You want to come? You'll make Mom feel safer."

He looked at me, weighing his options. He probably was trying to figure out if I was a better driver than he was.

I guess he reached a conclusion.

"Woof," he said eloquently and trotted beside me out the door.

I think I set a new speed record from San Buenasara to San Luis Obispo. No one stopped me. Where were the police when you needed them?

Karen was with Dean Matthews in his office. She was sitting, huddled in on herself, cradling a cup of tea in her hands. There were two big security guards in the office, as well.

She got up when Bruno and I came in. I put my arms around her. She was shaking.

"It'll be okay now, honey. I'm here."

Tears were running down her cheeks. I got out a tissue and gently dried them. Bruno leaned into her leg.

"Oh, Jimmy, I was so scared."

"I know, honey."

"Mr. Harris," Matthews said interrupting and extending his hand. I turned and took it, holding on to Karen with my other hand.

Karen sat down in one of the desk chairs, her shoulders slumped, and lapsed into thought. She seemed to be unwinding from the harrowing experience. Bruno jumped into her lap. She petted him absently. Her body seemed to ease.

"I'm so sorry this has happened," Matthews said. "Frankly, we've never had an incident like this. I've called the police, of course, but frankly, I don't think they can do much. I know they dusted the car for fingerprints, but there are no surveillance cameras in the garage."

"Dean Matthews, we appreciate your concern," I said. "But this may not be just a case of vandalism."

Explaining the situation to Matthews seemed like a good idea. This was serious and I didn't want Matthews to think Karen was overreacting. There could be other developments.

I had turned away from Karen instinctively, to spare her the embarrassment of my remarks, and lowered my voice.

"This has been a very stressful time for Karen and me. We are deeply involved in an election in San Buenasara and we think these incidents are related to that. There have been other threats."

Matthews was startled.

"Perhaps it would be a good idea if Mrs. Harris took a few weeks off, perhaps until after the election," Matthews suggested. "The semester is not too far along and she can start a new semester in January."

"I think that is a good idea," I said. "We can look after her better at home."

We both jumped when Karen hit Matthews' desk with her fist. Bruno gave a yelp and jumped off Karen's lap.

"No, damn it. It's happening again," she shouted angrily.

That took me completely by surprise.

"I'm sorry, darling. Did I say something?"

"I won't let them do it!"

"Who? Do what?"

"My mother. All of them. I just won't."

I was lost.

Karen straightened her back and squared her shoulders. Bruno was looking up at her, concerned.

"Jimmy, I don't want to quit again. I want to take my exams and I want to get this degree. I don't want to leave."

"Honey, you wouldn't be quitting. It would be just a few months."

"It feels like quitting." Her lips etched a thin wire across her mouth. Her eyes were hard, but unfocused, like she was seeing something I couldn't see.

"Mrs. Harris," Matthews said quickly, "if you want to continue, I can make one of our security people available to you when you are in class. He could also see you to and from your car. You can use my parking space. It is immediately outside the door."

"We could have someone ride in with you from San Buenasara."

"Jimmy, I don't think all that's necessary," she said, refocusing.

"Probably not. I only think they're trying to scare us." I hoped. "But it will make me feel better. And I need to figure out how to get someone to put a stop to this."

What I needed to do was talk to Clyde. He would figure it out.

Chapter 26

It was 8:00 the next night. I was home alone. Karen and Bruno were out at a rally.

Karen had insisted on going without me. She really was quite a lady. Pamela had offered to drive over with her so she wouldn't be alone.

Clyde and I hadn't been able to talk. He had been in Los Angeles at a hearing and had stayed over.

I was home, deep in thought about the next step in our campaign strategy and how to stop Carsone. The more cynical of you might say that I was asleep on the couch in our upstairs bedroom, but you have not experienced deep meditation, of which I am a master. I always wear my pajamas when I meditate.

The ringing of the doorbell startled me. We don't get many visitors late in the evening. I rolled off the couch and stood up a little too fast. I staggered to the stairs and made my way down them slowly, gripping the rail. It is only 20 feet from the bottom of the stairs to the front door. The doorbell rang again, angrily.

"I'm coming," I yelled from the staircase.

We don't have a big house, but I think one should approach the outside with caution. I looked through the peephole. All I could see was darkness.

I stepped to the side of the door. Maybe I had seen too many television shows.

118

"Who's there?" I said it loudly and with authority. I thought that was pretty direct.

"Officer Sidney Jenkins of the San Buenasara Police Department." He flipped on his flashlight and held it under his badge. "Please open the door."

I did so. A light rain hit me in the face. Sid had one of those plastic covers over his police cap and a raincoat over his uniform.

"Hi, Sid," I said, opening the door. "Come in."

Sid came in and stood in the hallway. "Why all the formality?" I closed the door behind him.

Sid gave me a cheery little wave. I helped him out last year with a little credit thing. We were friends.

"What's up? Can I get you a beer?"

He drew erect and spoke slowly and clearly. He looked me in the eyes.

"I would like to speak to Bruno Harris," he said in a stern voice.

Most people don't usually ask to speak to Bruno. But there's a first for everything. I didn't know the game but I was game to try.

"He's not here at present," I said in a proper lawyerly tone.

"I have a warrant for the arrest of Mr. Harris. May I come in and view the premises?"

I nodded and stepped aside. Sid poured into the room. The room shrank back.

Sid is a big guy. Big people seem to occupy a room. With Sid, it was like the room just threw its arms around him to keep from exploding. When he played defensive left tackle for the Rams, before he blew out his knee, they couldn't find a poster big enough to include his head. Sid was in the ProBowl twice. He is actually the sweetest guy in San Buenasara.

"You're kidding, right?"

"No, sir. The Police Department is arresting Mr. Harris for indecent exposure and defecating in public."

I started to laugh. I couldn't help myself.

"For God's sake, Bruno's a dog. You know that. You can't arrest a dog for indecent exposure."

"Ex-Chief Carsone believes if Mr. Harris can run for political office, he should be held to the same standards as other candidates. He has sworn out a warrant."

"Sid, Carsone is the other candidate."

"I know. However, as a sworn officer, I must carry out my orders. I have been ordered by my Chief of Police to come to this house and arrest Bruno Harris."

"These orders came from our new chief of police? Mr. Carsone's nephew?"

"I am not at liberty to discuss police matters with a civilian."

"You want that drink?"

Sid's whole posture relaxed. "I thought you'd never ask again. A beer, please, Jimmy."

I walked into the kitchen with Sid trailing behind. I wasn't entirely sure he would fit in the kitchen.

"You know, this is the stupidest thing I've ever heard."

"Yep. Just doing my job. Following the orders of my leader."

"Bruno really isn't here. He's at a campaign rally with Karen. The 'Women Who Dog It' group. They're very enthusiastic."

"I know. I was there. I saw Bruno and Karen." Sid pulled out a chair and sat down at the little table.

I opened the refrigerator door. "Lager or ale?" I asked, surveying the contents. I looked back over my shoulder at Sid.

"Lager would be good, Jimmy."

I took out a bottle of lager and opened the drawer. I got out our bottle opener and popped the cap. I handed the bottle to Sid. I took out a glass and poured some Diet Coke for myself. I sat down across from him. We clinked glasses.

"Good to see you, Sid."

"The same, Jimmy."

"If you saw Bruno and Karen at the rally, why are you here?"

"Chief Carsone was very specific. I was to come to Bruno's residence and arrest him. I wasn't told to arrest him on sight. So that's what I did. And I thought maybe you'd want to know about the warrant."

I stood up. Sid picked up his beer and we went up the stairs into the living room. I thought we would be more comfortable.

Sid settled into one of the padded chairs by the coffee table. I swear the chair looked terrified. It squeaked in useless protest. I took a seat on the couch.

"That's great, Sid. I appreciate the heads up. I'll call Clyde. We'll quash this. And it will make a great story. People may die from laughing too much. Is Carsone an idiot?"

Sid took a long sip of beer before responding.

"Sir, I cannot comment on past or present members of the Police Department as a matter of policy." Sid said, pointing his index finger at his head and turning it in a tight circle.

"Of course," I said. "Quite correct."

"Jimmy," Sid said, turning serious, "I think Bruno would make a great mayor. Particularly given the other candidate. I'm a supporter. Can I make an anonymous contribution? I won't be able put up a lawn sign."

"Well, a contribution will help, Sid. It will mean a lot, even if you don't do a lawn sign. I'll personally tell Bruno about it when he gets back," I said.

I looked at my watch.

"I expect Karen and Bruno to be home around 9:30."

"I need to leave at 9:15. I'm on overtime and I wouldn't want to take advantage of my colleagues."

"That's really white of you, Sid," I said, which, in hindsight, might not have been the most politically correct thing to say to a black man. But he allowed me to remove my foot from my mouth so we could continue our pleasant chat, at least until 9:15.

Chapter 27

CLYDE WAS BACK FROM Los Angeles bright and early and in his office. When I found him, he was typing something on his computer.

I knocked on his open door.

When he looked up, I said, "Sorry to interrupt. We have a couple of emergencies."

He tilted his head to the side and gave me a 'go on' gesture with his hand.

"Someone attacked the Jaguar yesterday and scared Karen. And last night, they tried to arrest Bruno."

"Do tell," Clyde said, his words lifting at the end.

I related the incident with the Jaguar. Clyde was as concerned as I was. He wanted to consider how to respond. So we sat. The police were obviously a non-starter. He thought that trying to get the FBI involved would be difficult, but maybe not impossible. Clyde wanted to think about an approach.

Bruno's arrest was different. I think it was clearly the comic relief from all the drama.

"That has got to be the stupidest thing I ever heard," Clyde observed. "I'll get on preparing a writ. Should have it taken care of by this afternoon. Glad Sid warned us. Bruno might not like jail. You complained a lot when you were in jail."

The food was terrible. I thought I had a right to complain.

I spent the rest of the morning planning campaign strategy. It was too wet to go out. Later that afternoon, Clyde came into the conference room.

"Jimmy, I got hold of the papers Carsone filed to get the warrant. My friend at the court made a copy and emailed them to me."

"Good work." I'm always magnanimous.

"I have a hearing on our writ set for tomorrow morning." I watched as Clyde shuffled from foot to foot. He was anxious. That wasn't like Clyde. From the look on his face that there was something else and it wasn't good.

"Were there any surprises in the papers Carsone filed? Anything we should be worried about?" I looked at him quizzically in anticipation of his response.

"Well, no, not exactly." His answer was hesitant.

"Clyde, not exactly isn't an answer. What's doing?"

"It's the attorneys who filed the papers for Carsone. They worry me."

I raised my eyebrows. I've always wanted to be able to raise one eyebrow. I think it is cool. Karen can do it. I cannot.

"Why would it worry you? You're the best lawyer around."

"I'm not worried about them as lawyers." He sat down at the conference table and crossed his leg over his knee. He ran two fingers along the crease in his pants.

"Who are they?"

"Campion & Gilbert."

"What is Campion & Gilbert doing representing Carsone?" That was surprising and troublesome. This is a local election in a small town, a long way from LA. And Campion & Gilbert charges a lot of money.

"There is no way Carsone can afford them. I don't think they'd even take the job if he could," I continued.

"That's what worries me."

I knew John Campion from my former life. He had represented Guy Mason in his divorce from my client, the late Janet. He didn't like me. Why does that keep happening?

Campion & Gilbert is a large Los Angeles corporate law firm.

Last year, they offered Clyde a job. Thank God he turned them down. I'm too big a man to hold a grudge. I plan to grant them absolution next year, at the latest.

He turned down the job because he concluded John Campion was a pompous ass. It turned out that John Campion was more than an ass.

When I was President of Wee Willy's, our local pot producer, the FBI took it over. It was part of the mix-up when I was accused of murdering Willy. The FBI was concerned that a major Mexican drug cartel was laundering money through the company and they wanted to get the evidence necessary to indict them. They persuaded me to help them. Actually, they leaned on me so hard, I still walk with a tilt to one side.

The FBI discovered that John Campion was the business face of the cartel in the United States. He made the offer to buy Wee Willy's on behalf of one of the cartel's shell companies and delivered proof that he had signatory authority. He even bragged about all the deals he had done on behalf of his client and all the authority they had given him.

He delivered that proof directly into the hands of the FBI. And he also delivered the bank transaction details with the delivery of the purchase price.

The FBI served Campion & Gilbert with a subpoena of their records and Mr. Campion ended up in jail. Now, finally, he was a man of convictions.

Mr. Campion is still in jail, although I understand he has a pinstriped jump suit. The presence of Campion & Gilbert in Carsone's campaign raised a lot of questions.

Gino Bartoletti, the man for whom the Fire Plug worked, didn't have the money to fund a big real estate development project. He couldn't very well go out and apply for a loan. He was in the FBI witness protection program.

The Mexican cartel had the money. Was Campion still representing the cartel and directing this from jail? That thought was frightening.

"Clyde, I really don't like where this is going. I put my hand down on the conference table to keep it from shaking. "Do you think Carsone can be involved with the Mafia and the cartel."

"Jimmy, I have no idea what Carsone knows, or what he is ignoring. I do know that things have changed." Clyde's voice was emphatic.

"Do you think we should call the FBI?"

"Yeah, Jimmy, I do. Now, I really do."

"I'll get on it. I still have friends there."

I don't know why, but I thought Clyde gave me a funny look.

Chapter 28

"I NEED YOUR HELP."

"Mr. Harris, we are emersed in many matters of national importance. We are not a local cleaning service at your disposal," said Special Agent Marcus O'Leary of the FBI.

Special Agent O'Leary is my biggest fan in the FBI. He was involved with the Janet Mason matter. I know many more FBI agents than is normal or healthy. Special Agent O'Leary doesn't hate my guts, which makes him special. He even came to see me once on a personal visit. It was a few years ago and we haven't been in touch since, but a bond is a bond. At least he took my call.

It was early morning in San Buenasara. Early is a subjective judgement. It was afternoon in Washington, D.C. where Mr. O'Leary resides. I yawned and reached for my coffee cup. I was sitting at the Lilly Pad. There were only two other customers in the restaurant and I sat in our booth in the back near the kitchen. I had privacy. I also had a good cup of coffee which I cannot obtain at my office. I took a sip. Rich, good coffee.

Sure, it was raining. Not hard, but a steady mist. It seemed like it was always raining lately. Luckily, Karen had no classes today so I got to drive the Jaguar. We had gotten it back from Billy quicker than we had expected. Its tires were plump and its bumper unscarred.

I do love that car. Since Karen started law school in San Luis, the Jaguar and I had not had time to commune. I love the sweep of its bumpers and the smell of the leather seats. I like to hear the exhaust notes when the engine turns over. It can happen. It does sometimes.

I really needed Special Agent O'Leary's help. I sensed that he was hesitant to give it.

"I think the Mafia is trying to take over San Bucnasara," I said with a gravitas that is natural to me. I figured that would catch his attention. I put down my cup of coffee and leaned back against the leather booth.

"Ah, now I see," said O'Leary. His voice seemed to convey a sense of irony. They rode into town in black limousines with tommy guns. Is there blood flowing in the streets of San Buenasara. Do all their names end in a vowel?"

I had the feeling that I wasn't getting as far as I had hoped when making this call. Perhaps he wasn't grasping my point. I lifted my coffee cup to get a moment to think. It had gone cold. I waved at Lilly.

"Well, no," I said, "but I think they were involved in the murder of our local mayor."

"Mr. Harris, unless the murder involves a Federal statute, it is up to the state or local authorities to investigate. I thought you would know that as a lawyer. You are still a lawyer, aren't you. No more problems with the bar."

Special Agent O'Leary knows a great deal about some minor issues I had with the Bar many years ago. I still am sensitive about them. I continue to read the disciplinary section of the Bar Bulletin every month to make sure I haven't missed something. Like being disbarred.

I ignored the question.

"The police swept it under the rug. The Chief of Police called it an accident. I think he may have been involved. Now he's running for mayor." I didn't have any idea if Carsone was involved in the actual murder. He's dumb, but I didn't think he was that dumb.

The investigation was a different matter. Carsone could easily have diverted it. But I figured I should throw everything against the wall.

Lilly came over with the coffee pot. She even brought a fresh cup and filled it. I gave her one of my heart-stopping smiles. I think she staggered a bit, bless her.

I was doing a lot better with Lilly than I was with Special Agent O'Leary. He seemed to be a bit resistant.

"That's very interesting, Mr. Harris. Let me understand you. The police declared the death an accident. No state authority has become involved. There is no murder investigation, and from this you have concluded that the Mafia is taking over San Buenasara and murdered the mayor. What have I missed?"

He had it all wrong. I mean he had it all right, which was all wrong.

"But Gino Bartolletti is involved."

"Ah, I recall Mr. Bartolletti," O'Leary said. Finally, I had his attention.

"A fine witness, as I am sure you will agree," O'Leary continued. This was not where I wanted the discussion of Gino Bartoletti to go. "As a result of his testimony, we put some really bad people away and the FBI was able to bring justice to many hard-working citizens who were being cheated by the Mob's involvement in their pension fund."

The Gambrella crime family had been involved in the United Union Pension Fund fraud. The pension fund had been financing the Franklin Farms development in which my client, Janet Mason, was involved. Unfortunately, she was murdered. I think by Mr. Bartolleti. But the government, in its wisdom, put Mr. Bartolleti into Witness Protection in return for his rather lurid testimony about the operation of the pension fund. I found Mr. Bartolletti a person to be avoided. He terrified me.

I dug in with Special Agent O'Leary.

"But you guys let him go free. You need to help." A strong argument, I thought. Desperate, perhaps, but strong.

"Why do you think Mr. Bartolletti is involved? Have you seen him?"

"No, but you remember his enforcer? The one who looked like a giant fire plug?"

"Oh, you mean Seno Nesi. Yes, I do recall him."

Great. Now I knew the Fire Plug's name. I wasn't clear how that was going to help.

"Well, I saw him. He threatened me about the Carsone campaign."

"And Carsone is who again?"

"He's the Police Chief I told you about who is running for mayor."

"I see. And how does that lead you to believe Mr. Bartolletti is involved?"

"Come on. That was Bartolletti's guy. Someone is putting a lot of money into Carsone's campaign. We think the money is coming from offshore bank accounts. It must be Bartolletti." I made up the last part.

"Not exactly an open and shut argument, Mr. Harris. But, let me humor you. Even if it is Mr. Bartolletti, there is no reason he can't be involved in real estate development. It's an honest trade, more or less. It's good to see people turn over a new leaf. Don't you agree?"

"But, they're murdering people." I was getting huffy. I become huffy when I get frustrated. I get frustrated when I don't get my way. I know. It isn't exactly mature.

"Mr. Harris, I thought we established that no one has been murdered. And if they were, it's not up to us to become involved. I'm sorry, I have other active cases I need to attend to. Ones that fall under the aegis of the FBI." Then the line went dead.

That didn't go as planned. I needed to talk to Clyde. He would figure something out.

I discovered the problem with the Jaguar when I walked out the door. I had parked it half a block from Lilly's. I hadn't bothered to take an umbrella and now the rain was coming down in torrents.

Chapter 29

THE RAIN WAS BEATING a spirited tattoo on the roof of the Jaguar as I drove back to the office. It was having a better time than I was, but I found myself tapping my fingers on the steering wheel in time with the rhythm. Unfortunately, each time I nodded my head I got a drizzle of cold water down my neck. It had been a long half block from Lilly's to where I parked. I really had to remember to take an umbrella.

I got back, wet but unbowed. Pamela stopped me before I could go into Clyde's office. I sneezed.

"Bless you," she said and reached down beside her desk and handed me a small cloth towel. She had a dozen of them in a pile beside her desk. We had passed beyond the paper towel stage. I hate being so predictable.

"Thanks, Pamela. I have to talk to Clyde," I said it as I rubbed at my hair.

There's a special sound rain makes on a shingle roof. I hadn't been aware of it before. I suddenly was. I liked it. I don't know why, but I just stood there for a moment, drifting.

Pamela started to speak. She has a rather deep, gravelly voice. I reluctantly gave up listening to the rain and focused on her. She held up her hand with her palm towards me.

"Before you do that, Jimmy, you have to see this. I'm freaked."

She did sound freaked.

"There's a letter here from the Mississippi Canine Society addressed to Bruno."

Her concern baffled me.

"They probably just heard about the campaign. It's nothing to be upset about."

"Not to Bruno's campaign. I mean it's addressed to Bruno personally."

I didn't see the distinction, but then again, I was dealing with Pamela. "What does it say?" I thought that was a reasonable question under the circumstances.

"I don't know. I haven't opened it," she said, her voice rising. She held up the letter. It was still sealed.

"Why not?" I looked at her quizzically.

"Maybe because it's so weird. I get very bad vibes from it. You know, like dark emanations." Our receptionist has some off-the-wall ideas. I mean, why would the Mississippi Canine Society send Bruno a personal letter?

"Relax Pamela. It's nothing. Just give me the letter."

She handed it to me like it was very hot.

"They probably want to support Bruno," I said ripping the envelope open with my forefinger. That cost me one of those really painful paper cuts. "Damn," I said, sucking at my finger. I got blood on the letter.

I went on, a little angrily. "Maybe to endorse him, like the Friends of the Bruno Harris Dog Park did." I could see that. Bruno, the standard bearer. A hero.

I flipped open the letter and perused it. My eyes opened wide. "Wow."

"What 'wow'?" Pamela asked. "Was I right?"

"I have to hand it to you, Pamela, this is really weird, just like you said."

"What does it say?" Now there was an excited note in Pamela's voice. She straightened in her chair and leaned forward.

"Let me read it to you," I said.

Bruno Harris. We demand that you withdraw immediately from your candidacy for mayor of San Buenasara, California. To be identified as a politician is beneath the dignity of a dog. You are a scar upon the body canine.

We cannot countenance such a disgrace. This scar must be exorcised. It WILL be exorcised.

Please, for our sake as well as your well-being, repent before God visits upon you his punishment. Our prayers are with you.

"They capitalized *'WILL'?*" Pamela was responding to my emphasis when I read the word.

"Yeah," I said. Can you believe it? I mean I sympathize with them about being called a politician. No one wants to be called a politician. It's worse than being called a lawyer, although a lot of politicians are both. It's a burden.

"Aren't most of the politicians, lawyers, Jimmy?" she said echoing my thoughts.

"Well, that's true. But there are good lawyers." I was thinking of me and Clyde. Beyond that, I was unclear.

"I guess." Her eyes had a skeptical look, but she didn't argue. "What are we going to do?"

"Bruno is a brave dog. He wasn't afraid when he got death threats."

"That's another thing."

Pamela pointed at her desk. "You need to look at these."

She picked up a stack of maybe 10 letters, got up with some difficulty and leaned across the desk to hand them to me. Pamela is a large lady.

"Some of them are real nasty. I didn't like to read them."

"Let's see," I said. Pamela was right, some of the letters were brutal and vicious. What kind of people were out there. We all felt that Bruno would be okay if he got a lot of publicity.

That was probably true of the Carsone people. They wouldn't want the heat. But some nut? And there seemed to be more nuts out there than there were in a jar of Planter's Peanuts.

I didn't want to scare Pamela. She loved Bruno and she was very protective of him. And I wanted to talk to Clyde. My conversation with Special Agent O'Leary was even more problematic now. We really did need the FBI. Maybe I could argue it was a matter involving the Post Office. Even I didn't think that would fly.

"Don't worry, Pamela," I assured her. "Bruno's a brave dog. And no one wants Carsone as mayor."

Pamela nodded eagerly.

"We can't let that happen."

Pamela shook her head again, following right along.

"Bruno wouldn't want that. Even if he is branded a politician."

"Bruno has the best interests of San Buenasara at heart," I continued. "He loves this town. He has no interest in power."

I hoped I was right.

"If there is a good politician, Bruno will be it," I concluded.

But, to be honest, I had my concerns. If Bruno wins, he undoubtedly will want to sit with Karen and me at the dinner table. I'm okay with that. He practically sits at the dinner table with us now. It would just be a small elevation of his position.

I'm more concerned that he will want to sleep in bed with us. If he sleeps at the end, no problem. But he will probably want to sleep between us. I'm already worried that Karen loves Bruno more than she loves me. I could see I was going to have to set some ground rules with Bruno.

He is closer to the ground than I am. He has that advantage. But I'm a trained lawyer. Yeah, and he needs us. I mean, we are the ones who have to carry him over the finish line.

"We need to help Bruno get elected," I said bravely to Pamela.

"I'm not so sure how much he needs us," Pamela said. "Look at this other stack of letters."

She pushed a tall stack of letters towards me.

"And these checks." She handed me a bundle of checks that must have been an inch thick. I rifled through them. My eyes widened.

"And he has groupies," Pamela said, putting the coup de gras on my plans to reign Bruno in.

"You're kidding. Groupies?"

"They're calling themselves the 'Pups,'" Pamela continued.

I wanted to say something but my mouth was hanging open. Then I sneezed again. I hope I wasn't getting another cold. I really had to remember my umbrella.

"I saw one on Main Street yesterday. A girl with pretty orange hair."

It must have been during the half hour it wasn't raining.

Orange? I thought. Really?

"She was wearing a tee shirt. There were two large paws on the front of it. Over her breasts. The shirt said 'Paw Me.' She wasn't wearing a bra."

Who in San Buenasara would wear a tee shirt like that? I knew it was a silly question the moment I thought it. All the girls and half the boys.

"I was so embarrassed. The girl handed me a sheet that insisted I had to vote for Bruno and be willing to give my all for him. I never give my all, Jimmy."

You're telling me, Pamela, I reflected. I need to speak to her about that.

Instead, I said, "Pamela, I'm sorry Bruno embarrassed you. I'm sure he never intended to. His supporters are obviously enthusiastic."

"Oh, Bruno didn't embarrass me, Jimmy. I was embarrassed by how firm the girl's breasts were. She wasn't even from San Buenasara. She said she was on a pilgrimage from West Hollywood. She asked me where she could find Bruno. She had a strange smile."

God.

"You're kidding, right?"

"Un, un."

"I have to see Clyde," I said, making a lunge for his office door.

Chapter 30

CLYDE LOOKED UP AT me when I entered his office. "You look like hell." Sure, I was a little wet and my hair was all over the place. But I have a natural grace. I sneezed again. It was starting to feel hot in the office. I sat down opposite Clyde.

"Better take something so you don't catch cold."

Clyde was dressed in gray woolen trousers and a cashmere turtle neck. This one was a perky yellow. I wondered how many cashmere sweaters Clyde owned. His blue blazer was draped over the back of his chair.

Clyde keeps a dress shirt and tie behind his door in case he has to go to court unexpectedly. His hair is always neatly trimmed.

"Thanks a lot. The rumors of my death are greatly exaggerated." I put my hand to my mouth to stifle a yawn.

"I didn't know you could quote Mark Twain, Jimmy."

"Who?" I asked. "I've just had a hard day."

Clyde looked up at the ceiling and shook his head.

"It's not noon yet," Clyde said, looking down and raising his watch to his eyes.

"Some of us work harder than others."

"Right," Clyde said, drawing out the word.

"I'm tired," I said.

"Partying again?" Clyde was tapping his fingers on the desk. Clyde can be a wiseass. I don't know where he gets it from.

"Hey, I'm a married man. I'm not allowed to party." Actually, Karen does allow me to party, but only if it's someone's birthday.

"You're probably too old anyway."

Clyde paused and his face lost its smile. "But seriously, what's up?"

I adjusted myself to a more upright position in my chair and got serious too.

"I'm worried about Bruno. We keep getting those death threats. They are getting more serious. Actually, I'm scared for all of us after what happened to Karen. And I struck out with the FBI."

"Jimmy, all politicians get death threats. Most of those people who send them are just sick jerks. They're delusional."

"I know, but Bruno is doing well out there. He's getting more and more popular. It's crazy, but people are getting really enthusiastic."

I stood up and started walking towards the sideboard where Clyde had the coffee pot. Then I thought better of it and turned around.

"I'm scared for the little guy," I said as I took my seat again. "I mean, he's vulnerable. My God, they may try to hurt him. That's all it would take to knock him out of the race. It wouldn't be that hard. I mean that goon beat me up before. And it wouldn't even be that big of a deal. Not for someone like the Fire Plug or his boss."

Clyde nodded. He pursed his lips. "Understood. You could be right. We're not sure Bartoletti is involved, but we really don't want Bruno to get hurt."

"And remember, even if they hurt Bruno, the cops won't do anything. It's not like killing the mayor. Look how they handled that. And I somehow think the police are not going to put this on the top of their list. Not with Carsone's nephew being our new chief of police."

"So, what do you think we should do?" I liked it when Clyde asked my opinion. I put my hand to my lips and contemplated my response.

"We can't lock Bruno up," I said after thinking about it for a long moment. "We can't keep him here for the rest of the campaign. Carsone would win."

Clyde considered that. When he's thinking, Clyde has a kind

of odd, vacant look. The boy can think hard. He did a slow, 360 degree turn in his swivel chair.

"Well, we could get someone to guard him," he finally said. "But I don't know where we'd get the money," Clyde rubbed the side of his nose. "Even guarding him when he is out campaigning will be expensive."

"We've got some campaign contributions. Not a lot," I said. "Do you think it would even do any good?"

"It'll probably be enough to keep Carsone and his friends away, at least from the rallies. But there's still the real danger of poisoning. Enough to make Bruno sick. And we still have the odd nut job to worry about. Bruno is a curious dog and maybe not as up on real-world threats as he should be."

"That's why I still think we need the FBI," I said. "But O'Leary's not going to help. I mean, darn it, the FBI were the ones that let Bartoletti loose." I raised my hand in a gesture of frustration.

"Maybe you can give it a try," I said. "You got along pretty well with Tony Sturgis, didn't you?"

That drew a smile from Clyde.

"Why don't I call Tony," Clyde said. "Maybe I can get him on board."

Tony?

Special Agent Anthony Sturgis had offered Clyde a job with the FBI when we were involved with Wee Willy's. He hadn't offered me a job, but I thought that was just an oversight. Anyway, everyone offered Clyde a job. You'd have to be an idiot not to.

"Do you think he'll take your call?" I tipped my head slightly sideways as I asked.

"He did, last week."

"I didn't know you and Tony still talked." That was a revelation. I know I had a confused look on my face.

"Not that often. Every week or so. He's a great guy."

Just the way I remembered him.

"We need to be careful with Bruno until we figure out what to do," I said in my usual authoritative manner. "Maybe one of us will carry him while we are at the campaign events."

"Bruno will like that. Good thinking, chief. Maybe we should get him a bullet proof vest."

"Very funny, Clyde. But maybe Karen and I should get one if we are holding him."

That gave Clyde pause. He looked up and his expression turned serious.

"And no more treats and dog biscuits from the audience," I continued. "We can't take the chance they will be tampered with."

"Uh…. I think I'll let you explain that one to Bruno," Clyde said with conviction.

Why do I get all the hard jobs.

Clyde leaned forward in his chair and reached for the phone.

"Let me make the call to Tony," Clyde said, oblivious to my difficulties.

Chapter 31

"HEY CLYDE. GOOD TO hear from you. How're you doing?" Tony Sturgis' voice was round and welcoming.

"Great, Tony." Clyde was completely relaxed. He sounded chatty. It was pretty clear to me that he and Tony Sturgis were close.

"We hear you're drowning out there."

"Well, Tony, we haven't resorted to using boats yet. We may in a week or two. Most of us do know when to come in from the rain." Clyde gave me a meaningful look. Then he pulled out one of the bottom drawers in his desk and put his leg up, leaning back.

You'd think he would have more compassion. I took a tissue from my pocket and blew my nose.

"Did Martha finally get over her cough?" Clyde asked. I didn't know who Martha was.

"Yeah, she went back to school yesterday." The concern was evident in Sturgis' voice.

"No Covid?"

"Nope, just a bad cough. Thank goodness. Nancy and I were concerned," Sturgis said.

"I was concerned too," Clyde responded.

All the small talk was making me uncomfortable. I shifted my body in the chair and looked at Clyde. I made a little hand motion to ask him to speed it up. He shrugged. He picked up a pencil from his desk and started to twirl it between his fingers.

Outside the rain picked up and streamed down the window behind Clyde. The room darkened. Clyde put down the pencil and
leaned forward. He reached over and switched on the desk light.

"She's a great little girl, Tony. Both the kids are." Clyde's sincer-
ity was evident. He really knew the kids and liked them.

I had no idea Clyde and Sturgis saw each other. With his family
too. Wow.

"I love them, but they're a handful. It wears old guys like me out."

"Old guy, huh? I feel you, man. Glad you finally admitted it."
Clyde could kid an FBI agent. I was impressed.

"Don't have kids, Clyde. They'll wear you to a nub. I was a lot
taller before we had Martha and Rachael."

"I'll take that under advisement, Tony." He gave a little laugh
down in his throat.

"So, are you still working for the half-wit?"

Hey, I could hear Sturgis loud and clear. I had moved my chair
over to the other side of the desk, beside Clyde, and I had my ear
close to the phone. That was unkind. I mean, I resemble that re-
mark. I have all my wits about me, I just can't remember where I
left them sometimes.

"I am, Tony. In fact, Jimmy is here. Can I put him on? We have
an issue you maybe need to know about."

Finally!

"If you gott'a." Sturgis didn't sound exactly enthusiastic.

Clyde punched in the speaker button on the phone.

"Good morning, Tony," I said.

"That's Special Agent Sturgis, Harris. And you sound like shit."

"I've been working hard and I'm getting a cold."

"Come on, Tony. Play nice," Clyde chided.

"Maybe with you, Clyde. I still don't know why you didn't
come to work for me."

"Sometimes I wonder too, Tony. But Karen is really nice."

Traitor. I mean, I am the Senior Partner. Maybe reporting to
Karen and Bruno. But right up there.

"Special Agent Sturgis. The bad guys are trying to take over our town," I interjected.

"What, High Noon?" He grunted in a half-laugh.

"Well, kind'a."

"Explain 'kind'a,'" Harris," he said gruffly. All these FBI types have no imagination.

"Did you know that Bruno is running for Mayor?" I asked.

"Whose Bruno?"

"He's our long-haired dachshund."

"A dog?" He didn't seem impressed. Incredulous, but not impressed.

I told Sturgis about the mayor's death and the Police Chief running for Mayor. I didn't explain that we started to run Bruno as a joke. I thought that might take away a little of the gravitas.

"Do you know who Gino Bartoletti is?" I asked it as nicely as I could. I mean, FBI agents know everything, but I had to be sure.

"The union fund guy? Rolled over on some of his friends. We put some big bad guys away. As I remember, we put Bartoletti in Witness Protection."

"That's him. I think he killed a couple of people here. Janet Mason for one. We were really upset he got off scot free."

"That's too bad, Harris. I feel for you." I was pretty sure he didn't feel for me. I guess he doesn't know how sensitive I am. "I'm sure he will be punished in heaven for all his transgressions," Sturgis added. "But we got a lot more than you lost."

"I'm not trying to blame the Bureau," I hastened to say. God forbid. "Or second guess you." God really forbid. Never. Not me. "I just mean Bartoletti is a bad guy. A couple of days ago, Bartoletti's goon threatened me. We think Bartoletti is behind a major proposed real estate development here. There's a lot of money in this campaign. And there will be a lot of money necessary for the development. We don't know where that is coming from. There have been death threats against our candidate. We're scared."

"First, that seems like a state crime issue. Doesn't have anything to do with us." Sturgis' voice was clipped. I remember hearing that one before. "It's a shame it's not a kidnapping."

"Sorry."

"Yeah, now kidnapping is a crime we can do something about."

"You can?"

"Sure, but I don't think our authority extends to dogs. Or donkeys for that matter. Or the back half of horses."

"But this is about an election." I felt like this was déjà vu all over again.

"Yeah, but it isn't a federal election. I couldn't do anything if I wanted to. Besides, real estate development isn't a crime. I mean not legally."

"But they murdered the mayor." I noticed Clyde was growing fidgety. He was shaking his head at me and mouthing something.

"So? Report it to the local police," Sturgis said.

"But the police are running for mayor."

"Get the coroner's report and take it to the state police." His voice was dismissive.

"There's no coroner's report. The police guy whose running for mayor buried the investigation."

"It's still a state matter." Sturgis raised his voice in frustration. That wasn't good. I was starting to feel like I was pushing water uphill. And there was a lot of water around.

I was getting desperate. I leaned in closer to the phone.

"Do you remember Wee Willy's?" The FBI had used me as bait on their hook for that one. I was lucky to wiggle off with all my parts still attached.

"Sure. I had to deal with you for months. How could I forget. I still get nightmares. You were a pain in the ass, Harris."

That was disappointing. I thought we had worked together rather well. Special Agent Sturgis was the CFO of Wee Willy's. I mean he played the role of being the CFO of Wee Willy's. He actually ran the entire show, including me.

But at least I'm memorable. That's nice.

Clyde now leaned forward. He pointed a finger at himself, gesturing for me to let him talk, even though I thought I was doing a wonderful job. I reluctantly complied. I slumped back in my chair and folded my arms across my chest. I stuck out my legs.

"Tony, we think John Campion is doing the financing for Gino Bartoletti and running the legal end."

"That slimeball. I was delighted we put that arrogant prick in jail."

"We were too. But his law firm is representing the other candidate in the mayor's race and we can't figure out why. Unless, maybe Campion's cartel friends down in Mexico are financing the whole thing. It would be a great way to launder a lot of money."

"Give me some more, Clyde. I want to be sure I understand." The other line on Clyde's phone rang. He ignored it and went on. Clyde actually had Sturgis' attention. I put my legs back under me and leaned in.

"Campion's firm is doing all the legal work. We don't think his firm would represent a small-town police chief without a big push. He's not exactly the type of client a major firm wants."

"That's thin. I hate fucking lawyers." He paused. "Not you, Clyde."

I knew he was going to mention me next. It was on the tip of his tongue. He must have gotten distracted.

"Christ, I wish I never went to law school. I'm still trying to recover," he added.

"You're doing a great job in recovery," Clyde said, and laughed. "What step are you on now, Tony? Nineteen?

Sturgis joined in the laughter.

"I know it may be uncertain, but here's how I figure it." Clyde settled in to the steady, well-paced tempo he used in court. "I think it is compelling. And I think the FBI should be concerned. At least concerned enough to do a little digging. I'd like you to poke holes in it, Tony."

Clyde was good.

"Okay, shoot."

"When you put Mr. Bartoletti in witness protection, you changed his name, right?"

"Of course."

"And you confiscated his assets."

"Sure. Even the ones he was trying to hide."

"He wouldn't get in touch with former associates to fund this deal."

"Not if he wanted to continue living." There was suddenly a lot of loud sounds behind Sturgis' voice.

"Tony, we're not keeping you from something more pressing, are we?"

"No, no. Just some of the guys organizing to go on a raid. Not my section. Go ahead. You've got my attention."

"Well, Bartoletti has no assets or track record he could use to persuade a bank to loan him a lot of money."

"Obviously not. I don't think he would want to go near a bank anyway, if he has any sense."

"So how come a major law firm wants to represent an un-known policeman who is running up a major legal tab on a long-term deal? Exactly how is he going to pay?"

"I see the point," Sturgis said.

He paused. I could hear his breathing.

"You know, Clyde, you still should come to work for me. You would be a great investigator."

I shivered. It wasn't cold in here.

"Thanks, Tony. Not today. Maybe tomorrow."

My blood froze. Visions of poverty danced in my head.

"See, Tony, it all fits," Clyde continued. "Campion & Gilbert would not represent this police guy unless your prisoner John Campion and his Mexican Cartel friends directed them to do so. And everyone makes a lot of money with no visibility. No bank is going to loan Bartoletti money." Clyde's voice molded around the words. "But the drug cartel would, if Campion vouched for him. He knew Bartoletti from the Franklin Farms development. For all we know, he knew Bartoletti before that."

"I guess all that's possible," Tony Sturgis responded some-what hesitantly.

I had come up with the same analysis, but I wanted Clyde to get the credit. I have to remember to tell him.

"Bartoletti would go for it because there is no connection to his former Mafia colleagues."

Tony Sturgis didn't speak.

"Okay, let me get this straight, Clyde" he finally said. "You think John Campion is acting as a conduit for his friends in the Mexican Cartel to finance the development of San Buenasara after Gino Bartoletti puts in a new mayor and City Council."

"Right. Can you make some inquiries?" Clyde said casually. "I mean you don't want one of your prisoners running a criminal enterprise from a federal jail."

"Yeah, Clyde. I guess I can do that. John Campion was an even bigger asshole than your boss, if you can believe it."

Chapter 32

"WHERE'S BRUNO?" I SAID, suddenly aware that something wasn't right.

It was one of our rare, quiet evenings at home. There was a fire in the fireplace. We were sitting in the padded armchairs we liked to pull close to the fire. It wasn't even raining. There was a large, yellow moon shining in through the bedroom window.

I must have said it louder than I intended. Karen jumped.

"What?" she said, her voice rising.

"I let him out in the back yard. He gave me that look. His 'I need some privacy so I can take care of my natural needs' look. It seems like he's been out there a long time."

I walked over to the window that overlooked the backyard and raised the sash. "Bruno," I called.

I couldn't see anything but lawn. I leaned out to get a better view. I still didn't see Bruno. Nor did I sense any movement.

"He usually barks when he wants to come back in. I wonder what he's up to?" Karen said, still unconcerned.

"I'm going to go downstairs," I said. My anxiety was rising and I think Karen heard it in my voice.

"Let me grab a towel," she said, getting up and walking into the bathroom. She is always thinking ahead. "It's muddy." The ground was still saturated from the rain. "We'll need to wipe Bruno's feet."

"Good idea," I answered, although his feet weren't what I was concerned about.

"Maybe he likes being outside. He's had a lot of people stuff with this campaigning," Karen continued, as we made our way down the steps. There had been three campaign events in the last week. "Bruno's a ham. He loves the attention, but he looked tired."

"Yeah. He has seemed less perky. Maybe we need to slow down a little."

Karen and I were home alone, I mean alone with Bruno, for the first time in three weeks. We were enjoying just sitting by the fire and watching television. Karen was wearing blue jeans and a tee shirt. I was in my underwear and a robe.

Between law school classes and campaign events, Karen had been running herself ragged. She appeared to have gotten over the scare at the law school. The driver and the security guards had helped, I think. She was doing campaign events separately so I could get other things done.

Time seemed to be running short and there were a lot of things to do, including stuff like buying groceries so we didn't starve to death. The kind of enthusiasm Bruno was generating at his rallies was amazing to us. There had not been any further incidents, for which I was grateful.

I had some campaign events too, but I wasn't as beat as Karen. I more or less was walking myself ragged. Thank goodness the election was only a month away. We couldn't keep up this pace forever.

"Let's go let him in," Karen said.

I gathered my robe around me and retied it. Then Karen and I went down the stairs and walked through the kitchen to the back door. We have a little back yard with a 6-foot wooden fence around it. Karen had planted it with grass and flowers. It's not that Bruno could hide. There was a nearly full moon. I could see the entire yard.

It was cool in the open air. A breeze off the water caused me to pull the robe tighter as I looked around.

"Karen, he's gone." I raised my voice.

"Let's be calm, Jimmy. You know how curious Bruno is. Maybe he dug a hole under the fence and went exploring."

"He's never done that before."

Oh my God. He never runs away. Something's wrong.

I slipped on a pair of sandals I left by the door and went ginger-ly out into the yard trying to avoid the muddy areas. Karen stayed on the back step. It was obvious that Bruno wasn't there.

I traced the wall, pulling back bushes and clumps of flowers, soaking myself with rain water. Near the back corner, where the fence ran along the road in front of the marina, there was a hole. Not a hole under the fence. A hole in the fence.

I leaned over to get a closer look. I seemed to me like someone had kicked it in. Not a good sign.

"Karen, there's a hole through the fence here."

I moved as quickly as I could through the wet grass and muddy areas back to the step.

"Maybe you should leave those sandals out here," Karen said. And wipe off your feet." I always listen to Karen. I have to. It's a law of marriage.

"I'll get a coat. Let's take the car," she said.

We both grabbed jackets from the front closet. I didn't have any shoes, so I slipped my feet into a pair of rubber Wellingtons.

I have to tell you, I felt like a Bedouin in that jacket with my robe flowing out beneath it. A rather stupid looking Bedouin in rubber boots.

"Where are the keys," I said. "You drove the car last."

Maybe I was a little distracted.

"Jimmy, you're holding them. Calm down. We'll find Bruno. He's a smart dog. He'll be okay."

The thought that was running through my mind was the com-ment Special Agent Sturgis made about kidnapping.

I was reaching for the front doorknob when it knocked. The door didn't knock obviously, someone knocked on the front door, but I jumped. I may have yelped. What I know I did is step on Karen's foot.

"Ouch. Darn it, Jimmy, be careful."

She stepped in front of me and opened the door. Sid Jenkins

stood there, carving a huge hole in the night. He was wearing a ball cap and an open rain jacket, showing an old shirt and blue jeans. The white teeth of his smile lit him up in the darkness.

He was holding Bruno under one arm. Bruno is not a small dog. But Sid is not a small man. You would think a ProBowl offensive tackle would be as mean as a snake. I mean, people are trying to kill you out there on the football field.

Sid was as gentle as Ivory soap. He has huge hands. Bruno looked small. He was wagging his tail like crazy and trying to lick Sid's hand. Bruno likes Sid. That figures, because Sid likes Bruno.

"Sid, thank goodness. How did you find Bruno? We were just about to go looking for him," I said with relief suffusing my voice.

Sid leaned down and set Bruno carefully on the ground. He scratched him behind the ears. Bruno looked up at him. "You're a good boy," Sid said.

"Sid, Bruno's not a good boy. He ran away and scared the heck out of us."

"He didn't run away, Jimmy." Sid's voice was flat. It started to feather rain again. Bruno looked up and went inside. At least one of us knew when to come in out of the rain.

"Sid, come in," Karen said. "Let me get you something warm to drink."

"That would be great Karen," Sid said. "I'm kind of out of breath."

I did notice he was breathing a little hard, as if he had been running. I was the last in. Maybe you think that's a reflection on my acuity. I think it's my innate graciousness.

We all trooped to the small kitchen downstairs. Karen gestured for Sid to sit down at the table where we take our office breaks. I took another seat. She filled a kettle and put it on the stove. She boils water really well.

"I'll make you some hot chocolate," Karen said as she sat down beside us.

"Yum," Sid said as he shrugged out of his rain jacket and let it fall over the back of his chair. He placed his baseball cap on the vacant chair. Karen also slid out of her jacket. I kept mine on. I'm shy.

"Sid, what did you mean when you said Bruno didn't run away?" I asked.

"Some guy was trying to get Bruno into a car."

"Good lord, Sid, we're lucky you were around. Why were you here so late at night? You're not in uniform."

Sid looked abashed. "I been trying to stay around your house, Jimmy." He lifted his shoulders in a kind of helpless gesture. "There've been some rumors we been hearing down at the station. But I couldn't get the new Chief to make sure you were okay, so I'm kind of doing it myself, when I'm off duty."

"Sid, you should have told us."

"Didn't want to worry you. Besides, Bruno's my friend. And my candidate."

"That must not be very popular with the police. Particularly with Chief Nephew." The new police chief was a continuation of the line of nepotism that had lifted our opponent to the illustrious title of Chief of Police.

"Don't like that boy. Ain't good for the department. He doesn't like the idea of Bruno running against his uncle. Makes his uncle look like a dog."

Very funny. But Bruno would be offended.

Sid put his huge left hand down on our table. I swear it occupied half of it. The kettle on the stove started whistling. Karen rose to make hot chocolate all around. She brought a cup to Sid and me. Then turned, went back to get one for herself and rejoined us.

"Thank you, Karen. That sure smells good."

"Sid," I said, as he lifted the cup to his lips to blow on it, "did you see the guy who was trying to kidnap Bruno?"

"Not too good. It was dark. Had the car door open, but there was no light inside. Bruno was putting up a fuss. He had wiggled free and was barking like crazy. That boy's a fighter."

"We didn't hear a thing," Karen said. "Poor Bruno," she leaned down to pet him, "you were on your own." I swear Bruno was simpering. In the excitement, I had forgotten all about him. That was going to cost me. Bruno doesn't like being ignored.

"Probably too far away. Bruno got in a good bite. Guy was cussing and shaking his finger. That's what got my attention. I was on the next block, but I heard all the noise and came running. Guy was by his car, trying to get Bruno in. Bruno wasn't having any part of it."

"What kind of car was it?"

"Some kind of black Chevy."

"Did you see the license plate."

"Had mud on it. Guy jumped in the car and drove off when he saw me coming around the corner. Wearing some kind of mask on his head."

If I saw Sid coming around the corner, running at me, I would jump in my car too. Quarterbacks were known to faint at the sight.

"Jimmy, I gotta go," Sid said, drinking off the last of his hot chocolate.

"Stay a few more minutes, Sid. We need to figure out what to do. And obviously, we can't go to the police." I looked over at Karen. She nodded in agreement.

"Don't think you can," Sid said

"We can't watch Bruno all the time," Karen said. "I've felt like we're being watched when we take Bruno campaigning. You know, that feeling you get on the back of your neck."

"You never mentioned it," I said, turning towards her in surprise.

"There was no reason to. I wasn't even sure I wasn't imaging it."

"Do you think we should drop out of the race?" I asked.

"Not on your life. Not now." Karen is a fighter too.

"Then we need to figure out how to protect Bruno."

"The publicity from the *New York Times* article will help. They wouldn't want to hurt Bruno, I think. At least not so we would know." I hadn't thought about making him disappear. Carsone would just say he ran off.

"Should we hire someone like we got for me? That worked," Karen said.

"But not in a campaign setting, with so many people around, and going from place to place. Clyde and I talked about it. There would be too many people to track for one man. We would need to hire several and it'll cost a lot of money." Hey, I'm the campaign manager. That's my job.

"I'll bet we could raise it," Karen said emphatically.

"Maybe."

Sid shifted forward in his chair. It creaked in terror. Smart chair.

"Why not get a guard dog?" Sid said. "They've been real good in our department. I can find out where they come from."

"That's a terrific idea, Sid. Even one guard dog could protect Bruno. We only have to make sure the guard dog doesn't eat Bruno."

"That's a good one Jimmy."

"Sid, we can't thank you enough. You're great," I said, rising and extending my hand. Bruno rose too and wagged.

"It's all good Jimmy." Sid heaved himself up and dragged on his coat. He leaned down to pet Bruno.

"What a good guy," I said as the door closed behind him. "We need to do something special for him."

"He's had it rough," Karen agreed.

"Yeah, he was a terrific football player until he got hurt. I understand he didn't have very much money left. I guess he lived pretty high back then. To go from fame like that to nothing, so quickly. That must have been hard."

"I wonder how he reconciles those days with these," Karen said.

"He seems pretty happy."

"I hope so."

Karen's the good one in the family.

Chapter 33

THERE WAS A BOUNCE in my step, and I had a stupid smile on my face, as I tripped down the stairs for my commute to the office. I had had a swell evening with Karen. She lusts after me. I slept like a baby. I was as bright as a new penny. There were just three and a half weeks left.

I poked my head into Clyde's office to say hello. He wasn't there. His desk was clean and the lights were out. That's not right. Clyde is always there.

I retreated to the conference room and flipped on the lights. Unfortunately, the clouds were like a wet blanket over a good party. I was thinking about digging out my book of prayers to the Sun God. At least it wasn't raining.

I picked up my pencil and pulled my legal pad towards me. I spent the morning working on a speech for Bruno.

After two hours of vigorous effort, I was pecking away on my computer with two fingers to input the draft. I wish I had paid more attention to my typewriter in typing class instead of to the cute girl in front of me.

The speech was coming along. It's hard to write a speech for a dog, even a smart one. You have to get the inflections just right. I had just finished polishing an elegant phrase to a nice sheen.

The clouds seemed to tamp down the sound in the office. There was a tap at the conference room door. Clyde poked his head in.

At least I think it was Clyde. He would look like Clyde if he didn't have puffy eyes and day-old stubble.

"Jimmy, I need your advice."

Finally! Clyde must really be up against some tough legal question. Some obscure point about a Writ of Seizure or something. He needed the master. I was ready.

"Absolutely, Clyde. Anything you need," I said it magnanimously and gestured him to a chair. I didn't make him sit at my feet.

"It's about Sarah."

"Oh," I said, a little disappointed. Clyde pulled out a chair and slid into it.

Sarah was the nurse from San Luis that Clyde had been dating. Karen and I had met her a couple of times over the last year.

Clyde kind of grunted and leaned forward to put his hands on the table.

"You look like you were run over by Rusty's steamroller. Are you okay?"

"Yeah," Clyde said with a yawn. He stilled the yawn with a hand to his mouth and moved his head from side to side in short, sharp motions. "I just haven't been sleeping well."

"Clyde, what's the problem. You know we're here for you. Whatever you need."

I got up and went around the corner of the table. I put my hand on Clyde's shoulder and squeezed. "How can I help?" I said, looking down.

"She wants to move in."

That was unexpected, but it didn't prevent my masterly response. "Huh?" I said. But I said it with authority.

"She wants to move in," he repeated

"With you?"

Clyde gave me a hard look and a straight lipped shake of his head. I think he was indicating that I wasn't doing a very good job of connecting the dots. I went back and sat down.

"Remember, I told you that she was being evicted from her apartment," Clyde said.

"I think so." I mean, that had been weeks ago. I had a lot of things to store in my mind and limited storage.

"Well, I was helping her look for a new place last weekend. The apartment market is really tough now. There weren't a lot of places and the places that were available were awful. So, we went and had dinner. Then we went back to my place."

"Okay."

"When I woke up, I found her lying on her side, just staring at me. It's unnerving."

"It usually is." I speak from personal experience. I began to see where this was going. A lot of the difficult questions in life come up after having sex.

"I said, 'Hi.' She said, 'Why don't I move in with you.'"

"Maybe she was joking."

"She was dead serious and I may not have handled it as well as I could have. I couldn't think of what to say." Clyde rubbed at his face with his open hand.

My heavens, a lawyer whose tongue is tied. I better check our health insurance policy to see if it was covered. It was at that moment when the sun broke through the clouds and I was taken with the dust motes dancing in a beam of sunlight. I realized I wasn't terribly comfortable with this conversation.

"What happened?" I finally ventured.

"She got angry and left."

"What are you going to do?"

"Jimmy, if I knew that, I wouldn't be here."

"Shouldn't you be asking Karen about this instead of me?"

"Probably. But I felt uncomfortable. I thought it was more a man thing and you've been around a long time."

Thanks for that, Clyde. That makes me feel better. If only my rheumatism would stop hurting.

"And you had a lot of relationships before you met Karen, didn't you?"

Okay, I had a little experience.

"I like Sarah," Clyde said. He pursed his lips and gave a slight nod for emphasis.

"That's a good start," I ventured gingerly.

"We get along."

"Okay."

"I just don't know how to think about this. It's confusing. I mean a real relationship. I'm pretty happy now with the way things are. But, you know, Sarah is special. She's good looking and smart. We have great sex. How do you figure out what to do? I look at you and Karen and you have a terrific relationship. How did you find Karen? How do you make it work?"

I wasn't sure Clyde was old enough to hear the truth. How would he respond if I told him the answer to a good relationship was total subservience to your wife. I figured I better try to explain a little.

"Clyde, when you're young, sex is still exciting."

"It's not when you get old?" There was a fleeting look of horror that crossed Clyde's face.

"Yes, of course it is," I hastened to add. "It's just…different."

"How?" That was a logical question. I reached down and gathered my thoughts. That took a while.

"When I was your age," I finally continued, "I thought good sex was the key to everything. Nothing else mattered. We could work anything out."

"Sounds right."

"It isn't. You have to talk to a woman. In any relationship you'll be talking a lot more than you will be entwined." 'Entwined' was so much nicer a word than some others I considered. See, I'm sensitive.

I paused to see if I could make that clearer. "You remember your tort law?"

Clyde seemed to take a little umbrage at the question. His stiffened a bit.

"You remember the concept of 'but-for causation'?"

"Jimmy, I got an 'A' in torts." Truth be told, he got an 'A' in most everything.

That didn't stop me. "It's different than direct causation. You don't hit someone over the head with a stick. You knock over something that hits something else that knocks over something that hits the person on the head. Kind of a Rube Goldberg thing."

"Jimmy, I know what 'but-for causation' is," he said tartly.

"Good. Sex is 'but-for causation.'"

"You better explain that one to me, Boss."

"Look. Good sex can't make a good marriage. But bad sex can destroy it. Sex clarifies nothing. It pushes it down."

I thought Clyde was going to get up and applaud my extraordinary insight. Instead, he sat there thoughtfully. Undoubtedly reflecting on my sage explanation.

"You know, it's really hard living with someone, even if you like them a whole lot," I said, filling the gap in the conversation. I was obviously the exception to that rule, but why gloat. I think Clyde saw what I was thinking and rolled his eyes.

"If you live with someone a long time, it's tough. You grow at different rates. Each of you gets interested in different things and there's always sand in the gears."

"Hold it Boss. Sand?"

"Yeah, those things that keep a relationship from running smoothly. You'll never agree on the temperature in the bedroom. And she'll expect you to put down the toilet seat."

I know, I know. You can't believe Jimmy Harris is so smart. You're right, of course. But it may be because of all the mistakes I've made. If you get beaten around the ears enough, you learn something. Or you come away with very flat ears. It might even be the years I spent in therapy. I guess I was listening, even when the therapist wasn't talking.

"You're starting to scare me, Jimmy. I thought you and Karen had a great relationship.

"We do, Clyde. We talk a lot. Let me ask you something. Do you and Sarah laugh a lot together?"

He thought about that.

"Sometimes," he responded a little slowly.

"Does she get your sense of humor?"

"Sometimes," he responded again.

"I think laughing with each other is one of the most important things you can do together. Otherwise, this living stuff is really a downer. And kids are going to make it different. Harder. Your friend Sturgis warned you."

"He was kidding, Jimmy."

"I know Clyde. I also know they reshape the relationships in a family. They can distract from your relationship with your wife, or she can be distracted by them. Having kids is great, but they can absorb a whole relationship. Karen and I don't have kids, and it's still hard."

"You have Bruno."

"Exactly. He can absorb a whole relationship."

"So, how do I decide?"

"I guess first you have to think about whether Sarah is someone you want to spend every day with, forever. That's a long time. And give some thought to her hard edges."

"Why? Won't they wear down?"

"The sharp ones are not likely to change. Maybe they'll dull down. But they never really go away. The edges in either of you. Have you met her mother?"

"Huh? No."

"You've got to do that. It's likely to be her in 30 years. You need to know."

"Jimmy, I still don't know how to think this through."

"That's because you can't. It's not rational. There's one more thing you have to do. And this is the hard one. The only way you'll know is to give the relationship time."

Clyde gave me a puzzled look and an open-handed gesture.

"Clyde, everyone in any new relationship, is trying to make it work. We pretend." I paused at that one. It wasn't quite the right word.

"Compromise." That was better. "Often without acknowledging it. You might go to see a lot of rom coms. She might just love football. You need to spend enough time together to get to 'ordinary.' To be together long enough that you can't pretend anymore, even to yourself. So, my advice to you, lad, is move in together if you choose to, but make it clear that you've got to be together a long time before you'll think about marriage. Sarah may not like that. And that's the risk."

"But I have friends who got married after 3 months. They seem happy."

"Maybe they'll be lucky. Let me know in 15 years."

"You didn't wait three years."

How did he know that?

"Well, I was young. And lucky. But it has been rough at times."

Maybe I should tell him about total submission after all. Nah, why ruin it.

Clyde looked exhausted. I know I was.

"Thanks, man," he said. "I had no idea you were this smart."

Who knew? I certainly didn't.

Chapter 34

I WAS SITTING IN the conference room. It was about two in the afternoon. I was deeply contemplating strategic moves in our campaign. Pamela rushed in. She was flustered in the way she gets when the entertainment world intrudes upon our sheltered domain.

"Jimmy ... oh. I'm sorry. I didn't know you were sleeping."

She startled me. My eyes popped open and I sat straight up in my chair.

I didn't want to correct her. Allowing those who work for you to make errors is essential. It is the way they learn. You do not want to make them feel insecure.

"What is it, Pamela?" I said kindly. I yawned to put her at ease.

"*60 Minutes* is here." Her voice was almost jumping up and down with glee. I, of course, am used to celebrity.

"Ah, yes. We were expecting them." Since Scott Pelley had called, a succession of people had been in touch to work out the logistical details. Scott and I were now on a first name basis.

I had hoped, during the week, to find out what the FBI was doing, but Special Agent Sturgis had remained stubbornly silent. Clyde advised me not to call him.

On the positive side, there had been no other threats or attempts on Bruno. Maybe it was because of Rex. Rex is a massive German Shepard that Sid had arranged for us to rent through the police department.

I wouldn't want to tangle with Rex. Rex had a real presence and very large teeth. And he seemed to like Bruno, who made it a point of bossing him around.

My cold was gone. Karen had nursed me back to health. Sal had given me a swell haircut yesterday. I had on my pressed blue jeans and my blue cowboy shirt with the white buttons. My blazer was pressed and perfect. I had on my best pair of Justins. The ones with the great tooling. They gleamed.

And, I hadn't forgotten my umbrella often since Scott called. I was shined and polished for my debut on *60 Minutes*.

Nor did we forget Bruno. The groomer had done his job. Bruno's coat glowed and we had a brand-new red silk handkerchief that Karen had tied around his neck. Bruno seemed pleased with the handkerchief.

He and Rex were sleeping together under the conference room table. Rex had his paw across Bruno.

"Is Scott Pelley here?" I asked.

"Oh, gosh, no. It's someone named Jason Williams," Pamela said. He says he's the producer of the segment, whatever that is." She looked back over her shoulder towards her desk, leaned closer to me, and lowered her voice. "And he's got a lot of people with him." I have no idea why she thought that was a secret.

But I was rather disappointed that I wasn't going to have more time with Scott. In my experience, exposing others to my charm was very important. And fulfilling for them.

"Why don't you ask Mr. Williams to come in," I said, making an open-handed gesture. I thought about asking Pamela to make us some coffee, but I didn't think poisoning the *60 Minutes* crew before the filming was such a good idea. "Maybe you'd bring us some soft drinks and Perrier?" I asked. It was more of a plea.

Pamela nodded eagerly and left. She reappeared almost immediately. Our office is rather small. There was a man who looked to be in his late thirties or early forties behind her. I got up and extended my hand.

Williams didn't look like a producer. He was taller than I was and pretty trim. His close-cut hair was parted in the middle. He wore horn-rimmed glasses. His blue jeans were a little wrinkled and he had on an old shirt, buttoned to the neck. He looked more like an assistant professor at some small liberal arts college. The only thing unusual about him were his intense green eyes that seemed to take in everything around him. And he was dripping on our carpet.

"Mr. Williams," I said. I gave him my friendly smile. I save my block-buster smile for women. "I'm Jimmy Harris. Please call me Jimmy."

Bruno opened one eye, concluded it was not Scott Pelley, licked his nose, yawned and went back to sleep.

Williams took my hand and shook it. "Is that Bruno," Williams asked, looking down.

"It is. The man of the hour," I said.

"You mean, like the Nora Jones song?"

"Sorry, I've never heard of it," I said.

"Wow." His voice rose with his enthusiasm. "It's actually called 'The Man of the Hour.' It's great." Williams was obviously a Nora Jones fan but I had no idea why we were discussing her ouevre. "You have to get hold of it," he said. "She sings about all these great qualities in a guy. One who'll always love her and never leave her. Who'll not betray her. Someone who likes to cuddle at night. The song ends with a 'woof.' It's perfect for your campaign."

He was really excited.

"Wait a minute. I've got it on my cellphone. I'll play it for you," he said. He reached into his jacket pocket and pulled out his Apple phone. He punched some buttons, looked at the screen and punched some more. I couldn't do that. I had given up trying when I realized my smart phone was smarter than I was.

The room filled with music. It was, in fact, a great song. It was fun-ny, sweet and perfect. The only thing that was not perfect were the six people behind Jason who were shifting on their feet. But judging by the looks of resignation on their faces, this was not the first time they had experienced Jason chasing a wild hare on their time.

I reached for the pad I always keep on the conference table.

In case I have a great thought. It was blank, so there was a lot of room. I picked up a pen and jotted down the name of the song. We could use it at all our remaining campaign events. I mean, if Norma Jones would let us.

"Don't we have to get some kind of permission to use the song?" I asked.

"Yeah, probably," Williams said. Then he stopped. "But we did this segment on Nora last year. She and I hit it off. Maybe I can call her. I think she will get a real kick out of Bruno and the whole idea of a dog running for mayor. She has a wicked sense of humor."

"Jason, that's really nice of you," I said, noticing the puddle of water collecting at Williams feet. He noticed me looking.

"I'm really sorry to be dripping on you," Williams said. "Does it rain a lot around here?"

"Not really. But it rains a lot when it rains."

He nodded rather wetly. "Don't worry, we'll spread runners so we don't hurt your carpets and we'll clean up when we're done." Then he turned to the six people behind him.

I waved away his concerns with a gesture. When I looked around the conference room, I had a twinge. I guess I saw it differently today. It looked a little shabby. I hoped that wouldn't come through on television. "Let me introduce you." Williams brought me back to the present. "That's Jake, Hal and George," he said pointing at three guys standing in the doorway. They were a mismatched set. One was plump, one was very short and the last was tall and skinny. They all nodded, glumly. None of them responded to the introduction.

"They're our camera men. We use a three-camera shoot for our interviews. It gives depth and dimension to what we do. Craig, over there," he pointed to a younger man with flushed cheeks, wearing camouflage pants and a T-shirt under a denim jacket, "he's our lighting person. He's going to set up a lot of pipes and hang some pretty bright lights. He's good."

Jason paused and flashed a toothy grin. "And don't worry. We learned a lot from all the lights falling on Hilary and Bill. It hardly happens anymore."

He was kidding, I think.

"Craig will bring out the best in Bruno."

Hey, what about me.

"Steve does the audio." Williams nodded towards a young guy in wet blue jeans. "He'll have a boom mike that will get everything. But, if you don't mind, we'll put a small mic under your shirt to complement the sounds.

"Sure, that will be okay. It won't tickle, will it?"

"Promise," he said. Williams was looking around the conference room appraisingly as he spoke.

"And finally," he said, turning back towards his colleagues, "the pretty lady back there is Justine." She was a small girl, almost lost among the men. She stepped forward and offered her hand. Her voice was bright. "It is a pleasure to meet you, Mr. Harris." Her English had a distinct French accent.

She was pretty. She must have been about 28, slim and dressed in jeans. Her face was striking and her eyes were a luminous light blue. Not that I was interested, you understand, being a married man. But I'm not dead.

"Justine does our makeup. She'll dust your face with powder so it doesn't shine and touch up anything on your face that will show up on camera.

"We do not want you to appear as, how do you say it, Richard Nixon," she said.

How did she know about Tricky ('Would you buy a used car from this man?') Dick Nixon. Did they teach that in powder puff school?

"That is if you want her to," Williams added.

Since I'm perfect, makeup should be easy, if not unnecessary. "Great," I acknowledged, giving Justine my megawatt smile. I think she stumbled back, but she didn't fall. I might need to practice that some more.

"Well, Justine," Williams said, turning to her with a laugh and gesturing down towards Bruno, "you're going to have a challenge doing Bruno's makeup."

"Mai non, Jason," she said, kneeling down to pet Bruno. Rex knew a pretty lady when he saw one. It would be unwise to get between Bruno and a pretty lady. He got up and moved away.

When she scratched Bruno's side, he rolled over so she could scratch his tummy. Somehow, he got in his licks, as well.

"You are such a beautiful boy," she said gently, ruffling his fur. "We shall have no trouble at all making you more beautiful." Bruno put his nose in her hand. The boy has great instincts.

"Isn't Scott Pelley coming?" I asked.

"Oh, sure. It will take us a couple of hours to set up. Scott's a real pro. I've been doing this with him for years. He'll be here an hour before we start. That will be plenty of time for him to get to know you and Bruno. He'd done his homework. Like I said, I admire the guy."

"Well, that's okay then. How long will the interview take?"

"Oh, maybe two to three hours, depending upon how it goes and how Scott feels about it. We tape a lot of extra footage. There's a lot of technical stuff, but you don't have to worry. We're pretty good at this."

Williams lowered his chin and chuckled. "Actually, it's all digital, but we still talk about tape. Then we go back and edit it to fit in the 15-minute segment."

"Ah," I said, knowingly.

"You mind if we get started?"

I didn't.

Chapter 35

"I'm Scott Pelley," he paused, as he did so well, then went on with emphasis, "and THIS is *60 Minutes.*"

We were all gathered in the sitting room upstairs watching our segment air. Polly had joined Karen, Clyde and me. Bruno had a seat in front.

There was popcorn. I love popcorn. After the seemingly endless commercial break, the camera came back to Pelley sitting on a tall stool in front of a room-sized screen showing Bruno. "Jason Williams, Producer" appeared over Pelley's left shoulder, near the top of Bruno's picture. Pelley started to speak again.

"Frankly, I don't know how to describe our next segment. I was not even sure how I would conduct this interview. I have been covering politics and interviewing politicians for my entire journalistic career. There have been extraordinary moments and there have been terrible moments, but there has never been a moment as odd as this."

The camera cut to our conference room and panned around, holding for a moment on pictures of Bruno and his campaign slogans. And came back to Pelley, in our conference room, sitting in a high-backed black leather. The conference table and chairs had been moved to the back of the room, off-camera.

"We are here in the small beachside town of San Buenasara. It is up the coast from Los Angeles, about a two-hour drive, and a few miles below San Luis Obispo. For those of you who have never been here, and I assume that is most of you, it is … quaint."

I thought that had been polite of Scott.

"But in the last month, its name has become widely known. A hard-fought battle for mayor of this small town has made headlines. It also captured our attention. So tonight, I am in the campaign headquarters of Bruno Harris, who in the latest *New York Times* poll is shown leading his opponent, Walter Carsone, by a significant margin. It is a compelling two-man race. Well, that may be a misstatement, as you will see right after this brief break."

We had stopped the interview in our conference room at that point as well, not because there was a commercial break, the commercials would be inserted later, but because there were some adjustments to the lighting Scott Pelley felt were necessary. The adjustments had been made quickly.

Scott Pelley, Bruno and I sat waiting until a camera man held up his right hand and counted down on his fingers. Then he pointed at us. The red light on the camera blinked back on.

"I, unfortunately, do not speak the candidate's native language," Pelley said, looking into the camera that was tightly focused on his face. He was trying to present a composed demeanor, but the corners of his lips were twitching upward. "So, we have asked Mr. James Emerson Harris to act as our interpreter for this interview."

Pelley turned away from the first camera and shifted his body to face me. "Good evening, Mr. Harris."

The second camera was focused over his shoulder. It had been my network debut. Who knew what might come next.

We had rearranged the best of the posters lining the wall so they were behind Bruno and would appear in any camera shots. I thought that was clever. Karen was the one that suggested it, but I had the same idea. We also had the room repainted.

"Good evening, Scott," I said giving him one of my patented smiles. Not being a woman, he didn't swoon, but I thought he may have trembled a bit. "Please call me Jimmy."

"Jimmy, would you please introduce us to the candidate?"

"I would be happy to, Scott." I turned and looked down at Bruno, who looked up, giving us his best profile.

The camera tightened to a close up of Bruno. Bruno sat next to me on a square cherrywood table we had bought for the occasion. It set off Bruno's coloring. The table was slightly lower than the chairs we were sitting in.

I opened my hand towards Bruno. "Scott, this is Bruno Harris."

"Good evening, Mr. Harris," Scott said.

Pelley leaned forward and down, extending his hand to shake Bruno's paw. Instead, Bruno licked his hand.

I thought Scott Pelley looked a little flustered. I don't think a politician had ever licked his hand before. Other parts of his anatomy, yes. But never his hand.

"Woof," said Bruno. For a dog, he was quite the showman.

I used the remote to put the show on hold. "Anyone want something to drink," I said standing. I grabbed the empty popcorn bowl and retreated into our small upstairs kitchen. I returned with beers for Polly and Clyde and a Diet Coke for me. Karen had passed. I sat down and restarted *60 Minutes*.

The camera pulled back to include me.

"Actually, Scott, he wishes you would call him Bruno. He's not very formal."

I honestly think Pelley may have been left speechless. Fortunately, his ultimate professionalism took over.

"I think you will have to agree this is an unusual interview," he said.

I chuckled and nodded. I couldn't subpress a grin.

Swiveling his body back and looking into the first camera, Pelley continued, "You might recall the name James Emerson Harris from a story two years ago concerning an organized crime scandal. It involved the death of Janet Mason, a prominent television star, and a trial that brought down a major crime syndicate." He turned back towards me. "Thank you for your agreement to talk to us this evening."

"It's our pleasure, Scott."

Pelley took off his glasses and folded his arms across his chest.

He pressed the tip of one of the temples against the edge of his lips. He spoke in his mellifluous voice, leaning in towards me.

"First, Jimmy, I think we need to understand your relationship to Bruno. It seems wrong to refer to you as his master or owner. After all, he is a candidate running for the highest office in San Buenasara."

I looked down for a moment to collect my thoughts and confer with Bruno. Then I looked up.

"Actually, Scott, it's pretty clear to me that Bruno doesn't regard me as his owner and certainly not his master. Quite the opposite. I've always felt that Bruno has looked upon me as someone who is there to fulfil his needs."

Pelley smiled.

"But in any case, Bruno is really a member of the family. Just ask my wife, Karen." I was chuffed to refer to Karen as my wife. I liked the way it felt on my lips. I continued.

"Since I'm Bruno's campaign manager, I guess that actually makes me his employee. Oh, and, of course, I'm his spokesperson."

"Why is a dog running for mayor." Pelley's eyes widened and his mouth conveyed a puzzle. "Wasn't there any other qualified candidate?"

"We don't want to speak negatively of our opponent, Scott."

"That's very funny, but really this is unusual, to put the best face on it. A dog running against a person. And apparently doing well."

"When Walter Carsone announced his candidacy following the sudden death of our mayor, many people here were concerned that he didn't represent our views. No one else stepped forward to run. Many of our neighbors, and my wife," there, I had said it again, "and I, felt Bruno did represent those concerns."

I didn't think I should mention the steps the Carsone campaign took to discourage other candidates. I didn't want to think about the Fire Plug, who might have been balling and unballing his fists as this was airing.

It was still raining when we taped the segment, but the *60 Minutes* crew had covered the windows for the shooting, so there were no shadows or changes in the light.

169

"Jimmy, really. Why didn't you run if you were going to be involved anyway," Scott asked. That was one I was prepared for.

"Bruno was more popular."

"How can a dog represent the views of the people here?"

"San Buenasara is a laid-back town."

"But why should anyone believe that the ideas and policies you are putting forward are ones Bruno would agree with and not your own?"

"That's a fair question, Scott. But we have been transparent with our ideas and the policies we intend to promote and Bruno's supporters seem comfortable with them. Bruno is not only man's best friend; he likes women too. He wants San Buenasara to remain unspoiled."

"Unchanged?"

"No, unspoiled. We intend to promote the potential of our beautiful town." I paused and shook my head. "We want change. But we want it carefully considered so that those of us who have lived here, and made this our home for many years, still feel comfortable." I had no idea what I was talking about. But that didn't seem different than any other politician.

"So, you believe Mr. Carsone will ruin San Buenasara."

"There is a lot of money behind Mr. Carsone's campaign. We don't know where it is coming from, but we suspect it is from outside developers and others. We do not want them making our decisions."

"But Bruno is a dog." Scott Pelley raised one of his eyebrows. I was jealous.

"We believe Bruno is the smartest candidate in the race," I said that with a straight face. I actually believed it. "Our desire is to run a positive and uplifting campaign."

We had paused the taping again at that point.

"It must be getting warm for you under all that lighting," Scott had said. That was thoughtful of him. "We need some exterior shots. Let's take them now and come back to finish up."

"Great idea," I said. Scott Pelley took my advice.

They took some shots of me walking Bruno, or vice versa. That wasn't as easy as it sounds. It was raining lightly and we had to get everyone, and the equipment, packed into vans. We had gotten Bruno a red rain jacket. He was quite proud of it. They took shots of me walking Bruno in his red jacket into the Lilly Pad and Scott, Bruno and me sitting in our booth. Then we had to get everything and everyone packed up again. After setting up again in the conference room, Pelley resumed.

"Walter Carsone has said that this is a sick joke, and he also said some unkind words about you." He leaned back with a serious look on his face. The camera cut to me.

"He has stated," Scott continued, "that San Buenasara has been too long in the hands of those who have no view of the future and that this city needs strong leadership. Would you care to make a comment?"

"Scott, we are blessed to live in a democracy, where the people are allowed to vote for the candidate whom they believe will represent their best interests. The *New York Times* poll shows Bruno is ahead in this race. Does that seem like a sick joke to you? Bruno is not hiding. People know who he is and what he stands for. He is loved here in San Buenasara."

I looked down at Bruno. "Do you agree?"

After considering his response carefully, Bruno looked straight at Scott and stated with admirable brevity, "Woof."

Chapter 36

"JOAN, THIS IS THE third call I've gotten today offering me TV ad time for Bruno' campaign. What's going on? We've never advertised on television."

Joan Van Dine had called to introduce herself as the sales manager for KRNP, one of our local TV stations. She seemed eager, maybe even a little desperate. This had never happened before in our campaign. Had the world changed when I wasn't looking?

I was sitting at the Lilly Pad in our red leather booth with a view of the kitchen. It was Tuesday, around 2 o'clock and the place was empty. Lilly closes at 3:00 on Tuesdays. I needed to get away from the office. I felt like the walls were closing in. Clyde was working, Karen was in school. Pamela was missing in action. There was no one to talk to except Bruno, and he wasn't in a talkative mood.

When I feel like this, I like walking up to Lilly's and hanging out.

In case you were wondering, I took my umbrella, even though it wasn't raining. Mama didn't raise any stupid puppies. At least not ones who had gotten as wet as I had.

I had my phone tucked between my shoulder and my ear, taking notes and sipping a Diet Coke with my free hand.

"Uh…" She hesitated. She had a nice voice. Young, but still excited about being in show business. She was obviously trying to decide how honest she should be. "We've had some ad time open up recently."

That was interesting. My nose was twitching.

"But why call us?" I asked.

"Well, I thought it would be great for Bruno to have some TV ads. He's cute. He really looks good on TV. I could make you a super deal."

"I'm not sure TV ads are the way to go. We don't have a lot of extra money to spend."

"But now, Mr. Harris, your ads will have a real impact on the campaign."

"Why now?"

"Well, to be frank with you, it was the Carsone campaign that cancelled all the ads they booked. You'd be getting their space and we would guarantee you there would be no competing ads." I thought that was a cleaver twist since it was a two-man race, more or less.

But Carsone's cancellation of his television advertising was interesting. I needed to find out what was going on. Lilly had left half an hour ago so I couldn't ask her.

I motioned for Cynthia, Lilly's other waitress to come over with the check. I took out a $5 bill and left it on top of the check. Then, I got up, took my umbrella and proceeded to the best source of information available.

Obviously, I had to go to Sal's. It had only been a week, but I felt an overwhelming urge to get my hair trimmed.

It still hadn't started raining, but it was threatening. Fortunately, I only had three blocks to go. I walked with purpose.

As I came up, I looked into Sal's plate glass window. Sam Witman was in the barber chair with Sal leaning over him, clipping at the hair on the side of his head. Sam is the local carpenter. Everyone uses Sam. He does good work.

Benny Smits was waiting in one of the chairs along the wall. I was surprised to see Benny. I thought he had moved away for a job. Bob, the dog, was nowhere in sight.

I felt the first drop of rain on my head. It was a cold rain. I ducked through the door without even having to unfurl my umbrella.

"Hey, Jimmy," Sal said, looking up at the tinkle of the bell over the door. "It'll be a few minutes. Want anything to drink?" Sal had started offering soft drinks and Perrier when he raised his prices. That's capitalism for you.

"I'm fine, Sal," I said, taking the seat next to Benny.

"How's the campaign going," Sal asked, flourishing his scissors towards me. "Where's Bruno?"

"He's home, resting up for his rally tonight. You coming?"

"Sure am. We like Bruno, don't we, guys?" he said, including Sam and Benny. That drew grunts and nods.

Hey, maybe I could write off this haircut as a campaign expense.

The rain darkened the shop. Sal's old ceiling fan made its lazy squeaking turns, stirring the air. It felt kind of cold and damp. I zipped up my jacket tighter.

Sal finished with Sam. He snapped off the sheet and it made a satisfying pop. I guess that's something you learn in barbering school.

"Nice haircut, Sam" I said admiringly as he got out of the chair.

"Thanks, Jimmy," he responded as he looked at himself in the back mirror, turning from side to side. He seemed satisfied.

Benny got up and settled into Sal's barber chair. Sal wrapped the sheet around his neck. He clicked the blades of the scissors together a few times before raising the scissors to Benny's head. Sal started clipping, looking over Benny's shoulder at me.

"Have you heard the news?" Sal said.

"What news?" I had come to the right place.

The rain started to come down harder and I leaned forward to hear Sal's response. He raised his voice a notch.

"Had a guy in yesterday. Didn't know him."

Sal knew everyone.

"Got to talking to him while he was in the chair." Sal likes to talk while he works.

"Said he used to work for Carsone."

"Really."

Sam was heading for the door, snapping his rain jacket closed. He stopped and turned back towards us, a quizzical look on his face. We all listened to Sal.

"Said he got laid off yesterday, along with most everybody else. Needed a haircut to go interview for a job in LA."

"Did he tell you what happened?" I asked.

"Yep. Asked him why. Said the campaign manager told him they were closing down the campaign office. Going to run the campaign out of Carsone's house."

"Man, they spent a lot of money on that office," Sam interjected from the doorway. Paid me almost $5000. Seemed to have a lot of money, the way they were throwing it around."

Sal nodded, then continued.

"Guy seemed to think there were suddenly some big money problems the way the campaign manager was acting, slippery like." Sal stopped clipping Benny's hair and looked up, the scissors still poised by the side of Benny's head. "Said he was worried he wasn't going to get his last paycheck. The reason he was hurrying down to LA. Sure looks like Carsone's well has gone dry. That's good for Bruno, right?"

It was and I suspected I knew why.

I walked back to the office. Eight whole blocks in the rain. Drops dripped from the few forlorn leaves that still were clinging to the tree that bordered Main Street. Rain bounced off the sidewalk. But I had my umbrella.

I knocked on Clyde's door first thing. Clyde looked up. He seemed perky again. Maybe he had solved his problem with Sarah. After all, I had given him great advice.

"Clyde, I just heard Carsone shut down his campaign office and fired everybody."

"That doesn't surprise me, Boss."

My ears perked up.

"Tony called?"

"He did."

"What did he say?"

"Well, mostly, he called to tell me the FBI appreciated the heads up. He didn't want to say too much because he said there might be another prosecution."

Well, dog gone. No. Not gone. Bruno's here. It's a saying.

Clyde put both hands on his desk, palms down, and leaned forward.

"Tony said not to worry too much about Campion and his friends. He said Mr. Campion had been 'secured.' Tony seemed really pleased. Even said to give you his regards."

"What do you think he meant?"

"About sending you his regards?"

Well, I'd probably have to pat those down for concealed weapons.

"No, about Campion."

"I think he's put Campion in a hole so deep he won't be able to see daylight. And I think they are making noises the Mexican Cartel won't like. I don't think we need to worry about Bartoletti's financing anymore."

"Did he offer you a job again."

Clyde leaned back and swiveled his chair around so his back was to me. He was still and spent a long moment looking out the window before responding. Finally, he turned back.

"Jimmy, he does that almost every week."

Well, that made me feel better.

"Did Tony say anything about Bartoletti?"

"Yeah, he did. Said his LA office had a discussion with our friend Gino. You're not going to believe this, but when they told Gino what was going on, Gino was shocked."

"Shocked," I mimicked.

"Yeah, shocked." Clyde closed his lips and nodded in concurrence. "He didn't know about Campion's involvement and he never suspected there was any question about the propriety of the financing of his proposed investment." Clyde said it with a straight face. That must have taken incredible control.

"Did they ask him where he got the financing from?"

"Old friends."

"And they didn't press him?"

"Apparently not. You know they may need him to testify again. In any case, he was adamant about not wanting to be involved in any deal where there was the least hint of impropriety. He said he intended to focus on other projects. The FBI expressed their continuing confidence in him and sent him on his way."

"Wonderful. Just wonderful." I sat back, exasperated. I let my hands fall to my lap.

"Where do you think the Fire Plug is?"

"Well, Jimmy, I tell you, I don't know, But I'll bet he isn't here."

Chapter 37

"I GUESS WE'RE IN for a dog fight," I said brightly with a grin. Yes, it was a terrible pun, but I couldn't help myself. Clyde just grimaced. "I wouldn't believe Carsone had it in him."

"I don't know why you're surprised, "Clyde said. "I never thought he would quit. I didn't think he could."

It was early in the morning. At least it was early for me. Karen had gone off to class. Only Bruno, Clyde and I were left to deal with the crisis in our mayoral campaign and me without my breakfast. I did have a cup of coffee on the conference room table in front of me, but Pamela had made it. I was letting it sit there to see if it did anything disturbing.

"He really didn't have much choice, did he, when you think about it? He resigned as Chief of Police. His nephew isn't going to give him his job back. He's desperate. That makes him dangerous." Clyde was standing, looking down at the newspapers spread out on the table that represented the crux of our problem.

"Do you think he'll try to hurt Bruno?"

"No. I mean he's politically dangerous. The issues Carsone is talking about are real, Jimmy. At least some of them are. And they are real enough to attract votes, even to a candidate like Carsone."

I tightened my lips. I knew what was coming.

"We just got the latest poll numbers from the *New York Times*." He picked up the paper and folded it to read the numbers to me.

*As we promised, we are keeping you updated on the mayoral race in
the town of San Buenasara, the small town on the Central Coast
of California. The former Chief of Police is running against a dog.*

*While the dog has retained his lead in our latest poll, which
was conducted consistently with our prior polls, the race has tightened significantly.*

*An editorial note. As our readers are aware, every person referred
to in the New York Times, is addressed by either his or her title or as
Mr. or Ms. However, our editorial board has confronted a dilemma.
After a great deal of discussion and some heated debate, it has concluded that a dog should be addressed by his first name only. This
should not be regarded as any reflection on the candidate or any
judgement by the Times on the campaign or the election.*

*Bruno, the long-haired Dachshund, is leading Chief Carsone
by 2 percentage points, which is well within the margin of error of
our poll. 42% of those voters likely to vote have indicated that they
intend to vote for Bruno while 40% favored Chief Carsone. 18%
remain undecided.*

Those polling numbers blind-sided me. I never imagined that
after losing his deep-pocketed backers, Carsone would actually mount a campaign. It all started two weeks ago with another
front-page editorial in the *San Buenasara Journal*. While Carsone
might not have the money for television ads, the *Journal* was still
ensconced in his camp, tending the campfire.

Bruno wasn't providing much input to the discussion Clyde
and I were having. He seemed distracted. I knew this election
threat must be bothering him.

The editorial in the *Journal* was playing the same old tune, but
the tune had new lyrics. That was the issue, or in this case the issues, and that was the problem. I couldn't hum along.

*We ask you, what do you really want in this mayoral election? A
dog or a real candidate. It was a great joke, a dog running for mayor.
Yes, we all had a good laugh. But isn't it time we considered the*

consequences of actually electing a dog mayor.

We know that Chief Carsone is not beloved to some voters, although we do not understand why. But he is a real person, with a real plan. He wants to bring affluence to the citizens of San Buenasara. To have this city recognized for the wonderful place it is.

Chief Carsone wants to fix the streets, to improve city services and to reduce property taxes.

These are worthy goals. Why would anyone not want to make San Buenasara a better place for everyone? To have new, thriving businesses that contribute tax dollars. To have new jobs. To have people seeking to live here, to join us.

Walter Carsone has a vision for San Buenasara. His opponent is a dog. Really, what does it mean when you elect a dog as mayor? Can a dog govern? No. The real mayor will be James Harris. Do you want James Harris as mayor? We believe the answer is an unqualified no. And we believe so for many reasons.

Apart from the total failure of his character, upon which we have previously commented, examine what he has accomplished for the city. His hard work destroyed our first new housing development in many years, Franklin Farms, and the jobs and opportunities it would have provided. Now that land can never be developed. It is in the hands of a national conservatorship, part of an impenetrable bureaucracy that does not care whether San Buenasara prospers or dies.

And what did San Buenasara get as a result? It got a dog park named after Mr. Harris's dog, who is now a candidate for mayor.

If that is not enough, Mr. Harris is responsible for the bankruptcy of Wee Willy's, the largest employer in San Buenasara. Those buildings still lie vacant and deteriorating. There is no work there.

Mr. Harris will be a disaster for the city. Do not let the cute idea, actually the obscene idea, of voting for Mr. Harris's dog fool you. That, in itself, is a black mark on Mr. Harris's character.

We ask you to vote for Walter Carsone. It will be a vote for your future.

In our defense, we were running Bruno as a joke. We didn't

spend a lot of time thinking about the issues actually confronting the city. About the problems plaguing it on a day-to-day basis and what a mayor might do about them.

Services cost money. Filling the potholes costs money. Trash collection costs money.

Money comes from taxes. People don't like to pay taxes. That is what might be called a conundrum, which is a drum that is hard to beat.

"What are you going to do, Jimmy?" Clyde asked, reasonably I thought.

I hadn't the slightest idea.

"Let me think about it," I ventured. That is the reason Clyde found me lying on the floor of the conference room talking to Bruno when he came in the next morning.

Chapter 38

OUR JOKE WAS NO longer a laughing matter. People seemed to like Bruno. I mean, I like Bruno, but this is different. There was a real possibility Bruno could be elected.

This was going to take some serious discussion. I was Bruno's campaign manager. We were going to have to see eye to eye on the issues, or it wasn't going to work.

But I know what I know. I don't know what I don't know, but knowing that wasn't important here. Bruno had a chance. A chance to do some good. I wanted that. I wanted it a lot.

If that meant having a serious discussion with Bruno, then so be it. The little guy was the only thing that stood between us and everything bad that Carsone represented. But I knew this talk was going to be labored and nuanced.

So, I got about it. It was important to see things from Bruno's perspective.

Therefore, I was on my stomach, lying on the carpet in the conference room. I had my elbows down and my chin resting on my fist. I wanted to look Bruno in the eye. I would have been looking him in the eye if he had had his eyes open. I started the discussion anyway.

I know you think it's crazy to talk to a dog. Particularly one who is ignoring you. Well... it is crazy. But lots of people think Bruno is smarter than I am.

When you consider that Bruno lives in a nice house for free, with two loyal servants who feed him and wait on him hand and foot, without his ever having to lift a paw, those people may have a point.

He has the love of a good woman. I can't forget that when I asked Karen to marry me, I mean the last time I asked Karen to marry me, when she finally said yes, she asked Bruno first to see if he wanted to propose. Thank God he didn't want to screw up a good thing by getting married. He's one smart dog. I like to think his decision was better for both of us.

Bruno opened one eye.

"Bruno, there's a problem," I said. "Carsone is an idiot, but what he says makes sense, at least in some ways."

I knew Bruno was considering my words. He yawned expressively.

I kind of liked lying on the floor but it was starting to hurt my neck. I readjusted my elbows. There was a nice little breeze down here. I would have to try lying here again when I didn't have obligations to fulfill.

I suddenly noticed there was a peanut on the floor under the conference table, probably from our last meeting. I was immediately beset by a concern. Was Bruno slipping? There was a time when a peanut would not have enough time to warm itself on the rug. I was going to have to watch Bruno. Maybe he was just tired. I knew I was. I cleared my throat.

"I've talked to a lot of our friends. This town does need more services. I mean, look at the pot holes. There are some that could swallow a car. And a lot of septic tanks aren't working so well any more. Our own included. A lot of them are 60 years old. They may leak and pollute the ocean. We need sewers."

Bruno looked puzzled. I would have to try harder. We needed to agree on his position. I was getting a stiff neck. I rolled over on my back, lifted my head slightly and turned it in a circle, working the muscles. Then I rolled back again. When you are doing something important, you have to push through the pain.

"Lilly feels downtown needs to be cleaned up. City Hall needs to be painted."

Bruno agreed. He stuck out his tongue and licked his nose. He does that when he thinks I'm on to something.

"And don't forget about water. It's getting more and more expensive. A lot of business people are complaining. The town needs to do something."

Bruno looked at me quizzically. I knew he wanted my thinking on how to accomplish all this.

"We need more taxes. It's the only way to get the money to do what has to be done. No one wants to pay more taxes. No one in San Buenasara would tolerate raising taxes. Even the ones who don't pay taxes. What that means is we have to get more taxpayers. Better ones. Businesses that will bring jobs."

Bruno tilted his head. I changed my position to adjust to his.

"Maybe we can use a little change, a little development. We don't have to change who we are or what we love about San Buenasara. Maybe a new hotel on the Pointe. Bed taxes are good money."

I paused to let that sink in.

"Maybe even a car dealership on the outskirts of town. Car dealerships bring in a lot of sales tax. Even some neat boutique business like Paolo's new restaurant."

I saw a look of agreement in Bruno's eyes. He lowered his chin. I could see that he saw the logic in what I was saying.

As he was about to respond, the door opened and Clyde walked in and looked down. His jaw dropped. He gawked at me.

Darn it, I would expect Clyde to understand. He stood there with his mouth open. Then he shook his head and walked out muttering something to himself. He closed the door carefully.

When I looked back at Bruno, he had fallen asleep. That was okay. I knew I had made my point.

Chapter 39

THE NEXT TWO WEEKS were frantic. We went all in and all out. Bruno had to get out his message. I was over my latest cold and ready for action.

It was still raining on our parade, but we got in another rally at the dog park. Half the people there just wanted Paolo's cookies. I wanted Paolo's cookies.

Bruno canvased door-to-door in his cute little red raincoat with Rex, his guard dog by his side, even when it was raining. Either Karen or I carried his umbrella. Since the Fire Plug had retired from Carsone's campaign, we weren't as concerned for Bruno's well-being, but we weren't letting our guard down either. You can never tell.

Reporters followed Bruno around, microphones extended like tramps extending their beggar's cups, firing questions. I think the questions were for Karen or me, but sometimes you couldn't tell.

We ran three television ads trumpeting Bruno's economic plans for San Buenasara. It was hard work, but now the campaign was real.

Carsone was out there to, trying to be an ordinary guy, shaking hands and kissing babies. That was an advantage. The more people saw of Carsone, the less they liked him. Bruno was more personable.

The only real problem was that Karen and I were both exhausted. Bone weary. We had been running in different directions for weeks. Karen was still going to law school full time. And campaigning full time. And we still needed her to run our law office. The only time I saw her was when we fell into bed at night, too tired to talk or do anything else.

It all came to a head two days before the election. We were in our bedroom.

"Honey, I'm sorry," I said. I'm good at that because I get to practice it so often.

"Jimmy, I was stuck for three hours by the side of the freeway waiting for the AAA to bring me gas." Her tone of voice made it perfectly clear to me that she was pissed. It wasn't hard to tell. Her hands were balled into fists and her eyes were squeezed tight.

"You were supposed to get the tank filled up. I missed my mid-term exam in Torts. That's half my grade."

"I got distracted. I'm really sorry."

She didn't seem assuaged.

"What can I do to help?"

"You can't do anything. That's the problem. I don't know how I'm going to get a make-up exam. It's going to really screw up my grades." She started to tear up. Karen doesn't do that. "I've worked so hard."

I stepped forward and hugged her. "Honey, we'll work it out. We're both beat. This election campaign has been too hard. I miss you."

"I miss you too, Jimmy. So much." She hugged me back. Then, she lifted her face to me and kissed me for a whole month worth of missing.

Two hours later we had a new outlook on the election, as well as plans for a post-election celebration. Bruno was going to get to celebrate too. With Pamela. He just didn't know it yet.

———————

Then, finally, it was election day. The sun was actually shining. There weren't even threatening clouds. It was weird.

Suddenly there was nothing for us to do except wait. Time hung like limp wash on a clothesline. All of the tension and adrenaline that had been pushing us was suddenly useless.

"Shall we get lunch?" I asked unenthusiastically.

"I guess," Karen responded with equal enthusiasm.

The time between lunch and the closing of the polls at 8:00 was endless. I felt like a teenage boy, waiting at home alone in the afternoon, for a hot date that night.

We tried to play Gin Rummy, but neither of us could get into it. Karen wandered up and down the stairs. Bruno was the only one who was calm. He exuded confidence. The boy has class.

People stopped by to wish us well. Polly came by late in the afternoon. He wasn't in any better shape than we were.

"I don't know," was his firm opinion, delivered with a rueful shake of the head before he left.

"Could we have done anything else?" Karen asked with a hint of helplessness in her voice. I couldn't think of anything more we could have done, except that I could think of everything.

I plopped into a chair in the bedroom with the book I was reading. Some silly art world mystery. I couldn't get into it and put it down. I was reminded of a book review by Dorothy Parker someone told me about. I thought it was funny, so I remembered it. Parker said of the novel, "This is a book not to be put lightly aside. It should be hurled from you with great force." I now saw the wisdom in that.

Pamela returned to the office, all excited. "Everyone's out voting," she shouted. "Everyone is talking about Bruno."

Karen and I came down stairs. Clyde came out of his office. He had been working with the door closed all day. His view was more centered. "It doesn't look too bad," was all he could muster.

Finally, the time ground down. We started to dress an hour early for the election party. We had decided on cowboy clothes. I had on my alligator boots and my best Stetson.

Karen was dressed in a cream colored, long-sleeve, silk shirt with French cuffs, over a short blue skirt with yellow stripes. There were antique enamel, twisted bull cuff-links inserted through the cuffs. She had on a wide belt with a large silver rodeo buckle and her blue Luccheses. Of course, she had on her cowboy hat. Win or lose, she looked terrific.

The groomer arrived. Bruno needed to look good too. Bruno gave her one of his suave looks as she picked him up and took him out to her truck. Bruno likes to be pampered.

Neither of us felt like eating. We piled into the Jaguar at 7:00. It actually started. That was a good omen.

Chapter 40

"MY GOD, WE WON."

Karen was holding the phone in her hand. She held it up in the air, raised towards us. There was a look of incredulity on her face. Along with a lopsided smile.

"That was Larry. He just finished counting the ballots. Bruno won by a landslide. He got 67% of the votes." So much for polls.

Karen and I were in the storeroom in the back of the Lilly Pad. She had laid her raincoat over one of the wooden chairs that surrounded a small square wooden table.

I had on my best blazer and wool gray slacks. My white cowboy shirt was completed by a string tie with a turquoise and silver clasp. I save it for special occasions. I looked good.

The door opened and Clyde came in. He looked even niftier in a dark blue suit that I swear looked custom-made, with a blue striped shirt with a white collar and white cuffs.

And, of course, the candidate was present. He was sleeping under the table. You had to admire his sense of confidence. We had the door closed. A large and exuberant crowd was milling out front. We could hear the laughter and shouts through the door. Bruno is the best sleeper I have ever known. Even better than me.

Karen bounced on her toes. "We won," she repeated to Clyde, doing a pirouette with her arms swinging with her turn.

The restaurant was the only place that was big enough to hold everyone who wanted to come. There must have been one hundred people crowded into the Lilly Pad. There were a half dozen reporters among the crowd and a television camera or two.

It was probably a fire violation, but the Fire Chief was at the front of the room. He had never been a fan of our erstwhile Chief of Police.

Lilly had pushed the tables aside again. People were overflowing the booths and crowding the space in the middle of the restaurant. Lilly had provided dips and little sandwiches. When we had offered to pay, she waved our offer aside.

"I want to get in good with the new mayor," she said. And that was before the votes were counted. Paolo had spent the last two days baking cookies. We had provided the beer and wine. Mostly beer. We knew our constituents. Our voters provided the other stimulants and the rich smell of pot drifted under the door.

"Why are you so excited? There was every indication we were going to win," Clyde said. That was somewhat different than his opinion this afternoon.

Karen put the receiver back into its cradle and smiled her great smile at Clyde. "Well, yes, but Bruno is a dog."

"I noticed."

"I mean people really voted for him."

"Yeah, I kind of got that too. At least 2,800 people."

"Hey Clyde, that's the most people who have ever voted in an election in San Buenasara. Bruno is really popular," I said admiringly.

"I love Bruno too, but we do have to wonder whether they were all high."

"Gosh, Clyde, that's unkind. I voted for Bruno. You know I'm sober."

"Jimmy, you're prejudiced. You're afraid of Bruno. That doesn't count."

"You voted for Bruno," I responded.

"Yeah, but Carsone is a menace."

"Where's Sarah?" I asked.

"Well," said Clyde, a little sheepishly, "I thought about all you said, and I decided that I wasn't ready to have a roommate."

Karen gave me a quizzical look. As she opened her mouth to say something, we were interrupted by loud shouting. There is a God.

Someone had announced the vote. People were yelling "Bruno, Bruno. They were laughing, stomping on the floor and making barking sounds. They seemed to be having a good time. Bruno was still sleeping soundly.

I had seen Polly out among the crowd when we came in. Everyone was patting him on the back. He was going to win too. Bruno's election was a very good sign.

"What do we do now?" I asked.

"Well," Clyde said, "I guess we should go out there," he nodded towards the door.

"That's not what I meant. I'm going to have to work with Bruno. What about our legal practice?"

"It'll be difficult, but we'll manage." Karen said it with appropriate reluctance.

Of course it will be difficult. I'm the heart of the law practice.

"We did it when you went off to run Wee Willy's." Clyde was trying to be upbeat through his apparent concern.

"Clyde, I went to run Wee Willy's because we didn't have any clients. Now we represent the city."

I brought that one in. I'm a great rainmaker. I even went to jail to bring in that client. That's what great rainmakers do.

"But this is more important than just a legal practice, Jimmy," Clyde said with a stiff upper lip. "Bruno needs you. You're his voice. His deputy. You can help a lot of people."

"I help people now," I said a little petulantly.

"But you'll help a lot more people by helping Bruno run San Buenasara," Karen interjected. "You know, when people were voting for Bruno, they were really voting for you," she said admiringly.

Well, maybe that was true. A little.

"You think so?" Both of them nodded vigorously. Karen put her hand on my arm and leaned over and kissed me.

"You will have issues running the city," Clyde said.

"I already have issues."

"When you have to make a decision, just ask yourself, 'What would Bruno do?'"

"It sounds like we're bringing in religion."

"Can't hurt," Clyde concluded.

"Besides, we need the conference room for the new paralegal," Clyde added it in an off-hand way.

"When did we hire a paralegal?" I asked.

"Two weeks ago. We've been really busy."

"Can we afford it?" I looked from Clyde to Karen.

"It's working out really well," Clyde said.

"Who did you hire?"

"Karen."

Oh, great.

"You know, Jimmy, we better go speak to all those people. I think every major newspaper and at least one network is out there waiting to hear Bruno speak. That is, if we can wake him up," Clyde observed.

After the Carsone campaign imploded and the Fire Plug fled town, towards the end of the campaign we concluded it would be okay to let his guard dog, Rex, return to his policing duties. He and Bruno had a tearful goodbye. So, Bruno was alone now. With us, I mean.

I picked Bruno up. He grumbled, but opened his eyes. I leaned my head down until my mouth almost touched his ear. "You go, boy," I whispered in encouragement. He ignored me and looked around for Karen. So much for loyalty and hard work.

I picked up my Stetson and put it on at my usual rakish angle. The four of us made our way through the kitchen. I always admired the way Lilly kept the place up. You can tell a lot about a restaurant from the places people can't see. The kitchen was spotless.

As we entered through the swinging doors to the dining room, all the cheering and foot stomping increased. People were jumping up and down, waving "This Town is Going to the Dogs" campaign signs above them.

Bruno looked over the crowd from his nest in my arms. He wagged his tail.

"I think he's enjoying this," Clyde said.

"Woof."

We walked up to a little platform at the end of the room. I put Bruno on the little table we had set up and held up my hands.

"Please."

The crowd yelled louder.

"Please," I said more forcefully.

As the crowd quieted, I took off my Stetson and cleared my throat. I could hear Nora Jones, "The Man of the Hour" playing.

As I opened my mouth to speak, Clyde stepped over and extended a microphone to me. "Thought this might be useful, Boss." I nodded my thanks.

Then I lifted the mic to my lips. "On behalf of Bruno, I can't thank you enough for your support. We always knew we might win by a nose, but this outpouring was completely unexpected."

There was more yelling. I waited for it to calm down. Boy, they must have had a lot of beer, I thought. They are really into this. They seem truly happy. That's great.

"If anyone doubts that San Buenasara is a town where all things are possible, tonight is the answer. Bruno was not, to say the least, the most likely candidate. Actually, we thought we were making a joke. But you saw it differently. Our campaign was built on you. You dug into your small savings and gave a dollar or two. Thank you for that.

"Bruno will be a great mayor. He cares about you. I have accepted the office of Deputy Mayor. I will be his spokesperson and the one who carries out his policies. But I assure you, Bruno's instincts will be the ones we will adopt and implement."

There were a few shouts of "Jimmy, Jimmy." Not enough to turn my head. I knew I was still working for Bruno. It wasn't much of a change.

"And since Bruno has chosen me as his Deputy Mayor and Spokesperson, he has agreed to waive his salary as Mayor.

Cheers.

"San Buenasara must move forward. We need to be better, but we need to preserve our way of life. I can't imagine not being able to party with you. Bruno feels even more strongly."

I pointed down into the crowd at Paolo, who was very near the front.

"Paolo Marino represents, in opening his new, world class Italian taverna, the kind of businesses we want. He did not tear down a house to build his new restaurant. He bought one of our old beachfront cottages and restored it.

"And he has promised to make his Bruno cookies. Ask for them when you go in."

Paolo smiled and turned and waved to everyone.

"We want small businesses, boutiques, that will attract people from all over. Perhaps a new hotel to put them up in. But we will not be overrun by tourists. We don't want to be another Carmel.

"And we want to use the money we generate to upgrade our police force. Bruno is going to start that process by naming Sid Jenkins our new Chief of Police."

Shouts of 'hoo, hoo' filled the room. People pounded Sid on the back, or as high up as they could reach. He looked astounded.

I held up my hand again.

"And we will address homelessness. We will find a home for Ben. He has had to live in his tent for too long."

And it might, incidentally, improve the looks of City Hall. I mean having a tent out front might not be the exact impression we wanted to convey.

Ben, whom I hadn't seen, put up his hand. "Hey, I like living in my tent," he shouted over the crowd noise. "I don't want to move."

"Gosh, Ben, we are going to find you a home you will love. Bruno promises you that."

"Well, okay then." Ben looked uncertain, but he seemed willing to try, bless his heart. What more could you ask. He might even get a job. Well, maybe not. Who knew. With a permanent address, he might even run for mayor.

"And finally, we are naming Lilly as our Director of Communications. She will be the source of everything you need to know about what is happening at City Hall. Lilly will keep us on the straight and narrow."

Someone in the crowd raised his glass and said, "To Lilly." Everyone in the room voiced her name.

"But, most of all," I concluded, "we want to know what you want. We may not be able to do everything, but we will sure do our best."

There was lots of applause. It's wonderful to be a natural.

A reporter held up her hand.

"Yes, please," I said, pointing at her and smiling. I caught myself and curbed my smile before she fainted.

"Your opponent, Walter Carsone, has just claimed the election was rigged. He says he doesn't know anyone who would vote for a dog. Everyone he speaks to voted for him."

"Mr. Carsone is certainly entitled to his opinion. If I had lost an election to a dog I might be upset too. Our election process is totally transparent. We vote and Larry Parson counts the ballots. His wife watches him carefully. She usually votes the other way. "

I paused for the few laughs that brought.

"No one has ever questioned Larry for the fourteen years he has been doing this. I don't think they will now. And it's not as if Bruno won by just a couple of votes. I think our citizens spoke clearly."

"Mr. Carsone says he intends to file a lawsuit challenging the election."

"We will certainly respond and cooperate with any investigation, although I suspect Mr. Carsone's out-of-town bankers may not want to finance that."

A reporter from one of the television stations held up his hand. I pointed and nodded to him.

"Is there any truth to the rumor that the FBI is investigating the financing of Mr. Carsone's campaign?"

"Golly, I hadn't heard that rumor." I gave him my most sincere look although I wanted to jump up and down and yell "Whoop-ee." "But the FBI isn't talking to me anymore, so I guess you'll have to ask them."

I cut off further questions. Everyone wanted to party.

"Well, thank you all for being here and thank you for everything. Bruno won't disappoint you, will you fellow?"

I looked down at Bruno.

"I guess you've unleashed the future," I said to him.

He raised his head and I lowered the microphone to him. He has a promising career as a politician. And I mean that in the best sense. He turned and looked over the crowd.

"Woof."

Acknowledgements

KIA MCINERNY AND GARY KUIST are lawyers. Kia is also a novelist. Gary is an avid reader and researcher. They did for me exactly what I hoped. They gently criticized, shaped and questioned my draft in detail. They suggested improvements. They added nuance. Kia and Gary were instrumental in the development of this book and I thank them.

My dear friend, Paul Tucker, is intrepid. You have to be intrepid to read and comment upon as many of my books as he has. Some may question his mental stability to be prepared to do so. But thank God. He is always insightful and generous with his time. His comments this time around were unique and thought provoking.

Tom Weinberger has read all my books and contributed greatly to my writing. He actually read the draft twice before he gave me his detailed and telling thoughts. His insights and questions on character and motivation were challenging and made me think. I cannot thank him enough.

David Rintels is an acclaimed playwright and screen writer. His three Emmys and six Peabodys shout his intellect and insight. I'm glad he's my friend. He took the time to read and comment on my draft. His comments were even more helpful than I had a right to expect.

And of course, I couldn't write a book without my wife, Anne. She reads, comments and encourages and has helped me become better. Thank you, Darling.

Made in the USA
Monee, IL
21 September 2024

65654311R00121